The Tragedy of the Korosko

ARTHUR CONAN DOYLE

The Tragedy of the Korosko, A. C. Doyle
Jazzybee Verlag Jürgen Beck
86450 Altenmünster, Loschberg 9
Deutschland

ISBN: 9783849690243

www.jazzybee-verlag.de
www.facebook.com/jazzybeeverlag
admin@jazzybee-verlag.de

Printed by Createspace, North Charleston, SC, USA

CONTENTS:

I

The public may possibly wonder why it is that they have never heard in the papers of the fate of the passengers of the Korosko. In these days of universal press agencies, responsive to the slightest stimulus, it may well seem incredible that an international incident of such importance should remain so long unchronicled. Suffice it that there were very valid reasons, both of a personal and of a political nature, for holding it back. The facts were well known to a good number of people at the time, and some version of them did actually appear in a provincial paper, but was generally discredited. They have now been thrown into narrative form, the incidents having been collated from the sworn statements of Colonel Cochrane Cochrane, of the Army and Navy Club, and from the letters of Miss Adams, of Boston, Mass.

These have been supplemented by the evidence of Captain Archer, of the Egyptian Camel Corps, as given before the secret Government inquiry at Cairo. Mr. James Stephens has refused to put his version of the matter into writing, but as these proofs have been submitted to him, and no correction or deletion has been made in them, it may be supposed that he has not succeeded in detecting any grave misstatement of fact, and that any objection which he may have to their publication depends rather upon private and personal scruples.

The Korosko, a turtle-bottomed, round-bowed stern-wheeler, with a 30-inch draught and the lines of a flat-iron, started upon the 13th of February in the year 1895, from Shellal, at the head of the first cataract, bound for Wady Halfa. I have a passenger card for the trip, which I here reproduce:

S. W. "Korosko," February 13th. Passengers.

Colonel Cochrane Cochrane, London.

Mr. Cecil Brown, London.

John H. Headingly, Boston, U. S. A.

Miss Adams Boston, U. S. A.

Miss S. Adams, Worcester, Mass. , U. S. A.

Mons. Fardet, Paris.

Mr. and Mrs. Belmont, Dublin.

James Stephens, Manchester.

Rev. John Stuart, Birmingham.

Mrs. Shlesinger, nurse and child Florence.

This was the party as it started from Shellal, with the intention of travelling up the two hundred miles of Nubian Nile which lie between the first and the second cataract.

It is a singular country, this Nubia. Varying in breadth from a few miles to as many yards (for the name is only applied to the narrow portion which is capable of cultivation), it extends in a thin, green, palm-fringed strip upon either side of the broad coffee-coloured river. Beyond it there stretches on the Libyan bank a savage and illimitable desert, extending to the whole breadth of Africa. On the other side an equally desolate wilderness is bounded only by the distant Red Sea. Between these two huge and barren expanses Nubia writhes like a green sandworm along the course of the river. Here and there it disappears altogether, and the Nile runs between black and sun-cracked hills, with the orange drift-sand lying like glaciers in their valleys. Everywhere one sees traces of vanished races and submerged civilisations. Grotesque graves dot the hills or stand up against the sky-line: pyramidal graves, tumulus graves, rock graves—everywhere, graves. And, occasionally, as the boat rounds a rocky point, one sees a deserted city up above—houses, walls, battlements, with the sun shining through the empty window squares. Sometimes you learn that it has been Roman, sometimes Egyptian, sometimes all record of its name or origin has been absolutely lost. You ask yourself in amazement why any race should build in so uncouth a solitude, and you find it difficult to accept the theory that this has only been of value as a guard-house to the richer country down below, and that these frequent cities have been so many fortresses to hold off the wild and predatory men of the south. But whatever be their explanation, be it a fierce neighbour, or be it a climatic change, there they stand, these grim and silent cities, and up on the hills you can see the graves of their people, like the port-holes of a man-of-war. It is through this weird, dead country that the tourists smoke and gossip and flirt as they pass up to the Egyptian frontier.

The passengers of the Korosko formed a merry party, for most of them had travelled up together from Cairo to Assouan, and even Anglo-Saxon ice thaws rapidly upon the Nile. They were fortunate in being without the single disagreeable person who, in these small boats, is sufficient to mar the enjoyment of the whole party. On a vessel which is little more than a large steam launch, the bore, the cynic, or the grumbler holds the company at his mercy. But the Korosko was free from anything of the kind. Colonel Cochrane Cochrane was one of those officers whom the British Government, acting upon a large system of averages, declares at a certain age to be incapable of further service, and who demonstrate the worth of such a system by spending their declining years in exploring Morocco, or shooting lions in Somaliland. He was a dark, straight, aquiline man, with a courteously deferential manner, but a steady, questioning eye; very neat in his dress and precise in his habits, a gentleman to the tips of his trim finger-nails. In his Anglo-Saxon dislike to effusiveness he had cultivated a self-contained manner which was apt at first acquaintance to be repellent, and he seemed to those who really knew him to be at some pains to conceal the kind heart and human emotions which influenced his actions. It was respect rather than affection which he inspired among his fellow-travellers, for they felt, like all who had ever met him, that he was a man with whom acquaintance was unlikely to ripen into a friendship, though a friendship, when once attained, would be an unchanging and inseparable part of himself. He wore a grizzled military moustache, but his hair was singularly black for a man of his years. He made no allusion in his conversation to the numerous campaigns in which he had distinguished himself, and the reason usually given for his reticence was that they dated back to such early Victorian days that he had to sacrifice his military glory at the shrine of his perennial youth.

Mr. Cecil Brown—to take the names in the chance order in which they appear upon the passenger list—was a young diplomatist from a Continental Embassy, a man slightly tainted with the Oxford manner, and erring upon the side of unnatural and inhuman refinement, but full of interesting talk and cultured thought. He had a sad, handsome face, a small wax-tipped moustache, a low voice and a listless manner, which was relieved by a charming habit of suddenly lighting up into a rapid smile and gleam when anything caught his fancy. An acquired cynicism was eternally crushing and overlying his natural youthful enthusiasms, and he ignored what was obvious while expressing keen appreciation for what seemed to the average man to be either trivial or unhealthy. He chose Walter Pater for his travelling author, and sat all day, reserved but affable, under the awning, with his novel and his sketch-book upon a camp-stool beside him. His personal dignity prevented him from making advances to others, but if they chose to address him they found a courteous and amiable companion.

The Americans formed a group by themselves. John H. Headingly was a New Englander, a graduate of Harvard, who was completing his education by a tour round the world. He stood for the best type of young American—quick, observant, serious, eager for knowledge and fairly free from prejudice, with a fine balance of unsectarian but earnest religious feeling which held him steady amid all the sudden gusts of youth. He had less of the appearance and more of the reality of culture than the young Oxford diplomatist, for he had keener emotions though less exact knowledge. Miss Adams and Miss Sadie Adams were aunt and niece, the former a little, energetic, hard-featured Bostonian old-maid, with a huge surplus of unused love behind her stern and swarthy features. She had never been from home before, and she was now busy upon the self-imposed task of bringing the East up to the standard of Massachusetts. She had hardly landed in Egypt before she realised that the country needed putting to rights, and since the conviction struck her she had been very fully occupied. The saddle-galled donkeys, the starved pariah dogs, the flies round the eyes of the babies, the naked children, the importunate beggars, the ragged, untidy women—they were all challenges to her conscience, and she plunged in bravely at her work of reformation. As she could not speak a word of the language, however, and was unable to make any of the delinquents understand what it was that she wanted, her passage up the Nile left the immemorial East very much as she had found it, but afforded a good deal of sympathetic amusement to her fellow-travellers. No one enjoyed her efforts more than her niece, Sadie, who shared with Mrs. Belmont the distinction of being the most popular person upon the boat. She was very young—fresh from Smith College—and she still possessed many both of the virtues and of the faults of a child. She had the frankness, the trusting confidence, the innocent straightforwardness, the high spirits, and also the loquacity and the want of reverence. But even her faults caused amusement, and if she had preserved many of the characteristics of a clever child, she was none the less a tall and handsome woman, who looked older than her years on account of that low curve of the hair over the ears, and that fullness of bodice and skirt which Mr. Gibson has either initiated or imitated. The whisk of those skirts, and the frank, incisive voice and pleasant, catching laugh were familiar and welcome sounds on board of the Korosko. Even the rigid Colonel softened into geniality, and the Oxford-bred diplomatist forgot to be unnatural with Miss Sadie Adams as a companion.

The other passengers may be dismissed more briefly. Some were interesting, some neutral, and all amiable. Monsieur Fardet was a good-natured but argumentative Frenchman, who held the most decided views as to the deep machinations of Great Britain, and the illegality of her position in Egypt. Mr. Belmont was an iron-grey, sturdy Irishman, famous as an astonishingly good long-range rifle-shot, who had carried off nearly every prize which Wimbledon or Bisley had to offer. With him was his wife, a very charming and refined woman, full of the pleasant playfulness of her country. Mrs. Shlesinger was a middle-aged widow, quiet and soothing, with her thoughts all taken up by her six-year-old child, as a mother's thoughts are likely to be in a boat which has an open rail for a bulwark. The Reverend John Stuart was a Nonconformist minister from Birmingham—either a Presbyterian or a Congregationalist—a man of immense stoutness, slow and torpid in his ways, but blessed with a considerable fund of homely humour, which made him, I am told, a very favourite preacher, and an effective speaker from advanced Radical platforms.

Finally, there was Mr. James Stephens, a Manchester solicitor (junior partner of Hickson, Ward, and Stephens), who was travelling to shake off the effects of an attack of influenza. Stephens was a man who, in the course of thirty years, had worked himself up from cleaning the firm's windows to managing its business. For most of that long time he had been absolutely immersed in dry, technical work, living with the one idea of satisfying old clients and attracting new ones, until his mind and soul had become as formal and precise as the laws which he expounded. A fine and sensitive nature was in danger of being as warped as a busy city man's is liable to become. His work had become an engrained habit, and, being a bachelor, he had hardly an interest in life to draw him away from it, so that his soul was being gradually bricked up like the body of a mediaeval nun. But at last there came this kindly illness, and Nature hustled James Stephens out of his groove, and sent him into the broad world far away from roaring Manchester and his shelves full of calf-skin authorities. At first he resented it deeply. Everything seemed trivial to him compared to his own petty routine. But gradually his eyes were opened, and he began dimly to see that it was his work which was trivial when compared to this wonderful, varied, inexplicable world of which he was so ignorant. Vaguely he realised that the interruption to his career might be more important than the career itself. All sorts of new interests took possession of him; and the middle-aged lawyer developed an after-glow of that youth which had been wasted among his books. His character was too formed to admit of his being anything but dry and precise in his ways, and a trifle pedantic in his mode of speech; but he read and thought and observed, scoring his "Baedeker" with underlinings and annotations as he had once done his "Prideaux's Commentaries." He had travelled up from Cairo with the party, and had contracted a friendship with Miss Adams and her niece. The young American girl, with her chatter, her audacity, and her constant flow of high spirits, amused and interested him, and she in turn felt a mixture of respect and of pity for his knowledge and his limitations. So they became good friends, and people smiled to see his clouded face and her sunny one bending over the same guide-book.

The little Korosko puffed and spluttered her way up the river, kicking up the white water behind her, and making more noise and fuss over her five knots an hour than an Atlantic liner on a record voyage. On deck, under the thick awning, sat her little family of passengers, and every few hours she eased down and sidled up to the bank to allow them to visit one more of that innumerable succession of temples. The remains, however, grow more modern as one ascends from Cairo, and travellers who have sated themselves at Gizeh and Sakara with the contemplation of the very oldest buildings which the hands of man have constructed, become impatient of temples which are hardly older than the Christian era. Ruins which would be gazed upon with wonder and veneration in any other country are hardly noticed in Egypt. The tourists viewed with languid interest the half-Greek art of the Nubian bas-reliefs; they climbed the hill of Korosko to see the sun rise over the savage Eastern desert; they were moved to wonder by the great shrine of Abou-Simbel, where some old race has hollowed out a mountain as if it were a cheese; and, finally, upon the evening of the fourth day of their travels they arrived at Wady Halfa, the frontier garrison town, some few hours after they were due, on account of a small mishap in the engine-room. The next morning was to be devoted to an expedition to the famous rock of Abousir, from which a great view may be obtained of the second cataract. At eight-thirty, as the passengers sat on deck after dinner, Mansoor, the dragoman, half Copt, half Syrian, came forward, according to the nightly custom, to announce the programme for the morrow.

"Ladies and gentlemen," said he, plunging boldly into the rapid but broken stream of his English, "to-morrow you will remember not to forget to rise when the gong strikes you for to compress the journey before twelve o'clock. Having arrived at the place where the donkeys expect us, we shall ride five miles over the desert, passing a temple of Ammon-ra, which dates itself from the eighteenth dynasty, upon the way, and so reach the celebrated pulpit rock of Abousir. The pulpit rock is supposed to have been called so, because it is a rock like a pulpit. When you have reached it you will know that you are on the very edge of civilisation, and that very little more will take you into the country of the Dervishes, which will be obvious to you at the top. Having passed the summit, you will perceive the full extremity of the second cataract, embracing wild natural beauties of the most dreadful variety. Here all very famous people carve their names—and so you will carve your names also."

Mansoor waited expectantly for a titter, and bowed to it when it arrived. "You will then return to Wady Halfa, and there remain two hours to suspect the Camel Corps, including the grooming of the beasts, and the bazaar before returning, so I wish you a very happy good-night."

There was a gleam of his white teeth in the lamplight, and then his long, dark petticoats, his short English cover-coat, and his red tarboosh vanished successively down the ladder. The low buzz of conversation which had been suspended by his coming broke out anew.

"I'm relying on you, Mr. Stephens, to tell me all about Abousir," said Miss Sadie Adams. "I do like to know what I am looking at right there at the time, and not six hours afterwards in my state-room. I haven't got Abou-Simbel and the wall pictures straight in my mind yet, though I saw them yesterday."

"I never hope to keep up with it," said her aunt. "When I am safe back in Commonwealth Avenue, and there's no dragoman to hustle me around, I'll have time to read about it all, and then I expect I shall begin to enthuse, and want to come right back again. But it's just too good of you, Mr. Stephens, to try and keep us informed."

"I thought that you might wish precise information, and so I prepared a small digest of the matter," said Stephens, handing a slip of paper to Miss Sadie. She looked at it in the light of the deck lamp, and broke into her low, hearty laugh.

"Re Abousir," she read; "now, what do you mean by 're,' Mr. Stephens? You put 're Rameses the Second' on the last paper you gave me."

"It is a habit I have acquired, Miss Sadie," said Stephens; "it is the custom in the legal profession when they make a memo."

"Make what, Mr. Stephens?"

"A memo—a memorandum, you know. We put re so-and-so to show what it is about."

"I suppose it's a good short way," said Miss Sadie, "but it feels queer somehow when applied to scenery or to dead Egyptian kings. 'Re Cheops'—doesn't that strike you as funny?"

"No, I can't say that it does," said Stephens.

"I wonder if it is true that the English have less humour than the Americans, or whether it's just another kind of humour," said the girl. She had a quiet, abstracted way of talking as if she were thinking aloud. "I used to imagine they had less, and yet, when you come to think of it, Dickens and Thackeray and Barrie, and so many other of the humourists we admire most are Britishers. Besides, I never in all my days heard people laugh so hard as in that London theatre. There was a man behind us, and every time he laughed Auntie looked round to see if a door had opened, he made such a draught. But you have some funny expressions, Mr. Stephens!"

"What else strikes you as funny, Miss Sadie?"

"Well, when you sent me the temple ticket and the little map, you began your letter, 'Enclosed, please find,' and then at the bottom, in brackets, you had '2 enclo.'"

"That is the usual form in business."

"Yes, in business," said Sadie demurely, and there was a silence.

"There's one thing I wish," remarked Miss Adams, in the hard, metallic voice with which she disguised her softness of heart, "and that is, that I could see the Legislature of this country and lay a few cold-drawn facts in front of them. I'd make a platform of my own, Mr. Stephens, and run a party on my ticket. A Bill for the compulsory use of eyewash would be one of my planks, and another would be for the abolition of those Yashmak veil things which turn a woman into a bale of cotton goods with a pair of eyes looking out of it."

"I never could think why they wore them," said Sadie; "until one day I saw one with her veil lifted. Then I knew."

"They make me tired, those women," cried Miss Adams wrathfully. "One might as well try to preach duty and decency and cleanliness to a line of bolsters. Why, good land, it was only yesterday at Abou-Simbel, Mr. Stephens, I was passing one of their houses—if you can call a mud-pie like that a house—and I saw two of the children at the door with the usual crust of flies round their eyes, and great holes in their poor little blue gowns! So I got off my donkey, and I turned up my sleeves, and I washed their faces well with my handkerchief, and sewed up the rents—for in this country I would as soon think of going ashore without my needle-case as without my white umbrella, Mr. Stephens. Then as I warmed on the job I got into the room —such a room!—and I packed the folks out of it, and I fairly did the chores as if I had been the hired help. I've seen no more of that temple of Abou-Simbel than if I had never left Boston; but, my sakes, I saw more dust and mess than you would think they could crowd into a house the size of a Newport bathing-hut. From the time I pinned up my skirt until I came out with my face the colour of that smoke-stack, wasn't more than an hour, or maybe an hour and a half, but I had that house as clean and fresh as a new pine-wood box. I had a New York Herald with me, and I lined their shelf with paper for them. Well, Mr. Stephens, when I had done washing my hands outside, I came past the door again, and there were those two children sitting on the stoop with their eyes full of flies, and all just the same as ever, except that each had a little paper cap made out of the New York Herald upon his head. But, say, Sadie, it's going on to ten o'clock, and to-morrow an early excursion."

"It's just too beautiful, this purple sky and the great silver stars," said Sadie. "Look at the silent desert and the black shadows of the hills. It's grand, but it's terrible too; and then when you think that we really are, as that dragoman said just now, on the very end of civilisation, and with nothing but savagery and bloodshed down there where the Southern Cross is twinkling so prettily, why, it's like standing on the beautiful edge of a live volcano."

"Shucks, Sadie, don't talk like that, child," said the older woman nervously. "It's enough to scare any one to listen to you."

"Well, but don't you feel it yourself, Auntie? Look at that great desert stretching away and away until it is lost in the shadows. Hear the sad whisper of the wind across it! It's just the most solemn thing that ever I saw in my life."

"I'm glad we've found something that will make you solemn, my dear," said her Aunt. "I've sometimes thought—Sakes alive, what's that?"

From somewhere amongst the hill shadows upon the other side of the river there had risen a high shrill whimpering, rising and swelling, to end in a long weary wail.

"It's only a jackal, Miss Adams," said Stephens. "I heard one when we went out to see the Sphinx by moonlight."

But the American lady had risen, and her face showed that her nerves had been ruffled.

"If I had my time over again I wouldn't have come past Assouan," said she. "I can't think what possessed me to bring you all the way up here, Sadie. Your mother will think that I am clean crazy, and I'd never dare to look her in the eye if anything went wrong with us. I've seen all I want to see of this river, and all I ask now is to be back at Cairo again."

"Why, Auntie," cried the girl, "it isn't like you to be faint-hearted. "

"Well, I don't know how it is, Sadie, but I feel a bit unstrung, and that beast caterwauling over yonder was just more than I could put up with. There's one consolation, we are scheduled to be on our way home to-morrow, after we've seen this one rock or temple, or whatever it is. I'm full up of rocks and temples, Mr. Stephens. I shouldn't mope if I never saw another. Come, Sadie! Good-night!"

"Good-night! Good-night, Miss Adams!"

And the two ladies passed down to their cabins.

Monsieur Fardet was chatting, in a subdued voice, with Headingly, the young Harvard graduate, bending forward confidentially between the whiffs of his cigarette.

"Dervishes, Mister Headingly!" said he, speaking excellent English, but separating his syllables as d Frenchman will. "There are no Dervishes. They do not exist."

"Why, I thought the woods were full of them," said the American.

Monsieur Fardet glanced across to where the red core of Colonel Cochrane's cigar was glowing through the darkness.

"You are an American, and you do not like the English," he whispered. "It is perfectly comprehended upon the Continent that the Americans are opposed to the English."

"Well," said Headingly, with his slow, deliberate manner, "I won't say that we have not our tiffs, and there are some of our people—mostly of Irish stock—who are always mad with England; but the most of us have a kindly thought for the mother country. You see they may be aggravating folk sometimes, but after all they are our own folk, and we can't wipe that off the slate."

"Eh bien!" said the Frenchman. "At least I can say to you what I could not without offence say to these others. And I repeat that there are no Dervishes. They were an invention of Lord Cromer in the year 1885."

"You don't say!" cried Headingly.

"It is well known in Paris, and has been exposed in La Patrie and other of our so well-informed papers."

"Hut this is colossal," said Headingly. "Do you mean to tell me, Monsieur Fardet, that the siege of Khartoum and the death of Gordon and the rest of it was just one great bluff?"

"I will not deny that there was an emeute, but it was local, you understand, and now long forgotten. Since then there has been profound peace in the Soudan."

"But I have heard of raids, Monsieur Fardet, and I've read of battles, too, when the Arabs tried to invade Egypt. It was only Two days ago that we passed Toski, where the dragoman said there had been a fight. Is that all bluff also?"

"Pah, my friend, you do not know the English. You look at them as you see them with their pipes and their contented faces, and you say, 'Now, these are good, simple folk, who will never hurt any one.' But all the time they are thinking and watching and planning. 'Here is Egypt weak,' they cry. 'Allons!' and down they swoop like a gull upon a crust. 'You have no right there,' says the world. 'Come out of it!' But England has already begun to tidy everything, just like the good Miss Adams when she forces her way into the house of an Arab. 'Come out,' says the world. 'Certainly,' says England; 'just wait one little minute until I have made everything nice and proper. 'So the world waits for a year or so, and then it says once again, 'Come out. ' 'Just wait a little,' says England; 'there is trouble at Khartoum, and when I have set that all right I shall be very glad to come out.' So they wait until it is all over, and then again they say, 'Come out.' 'How can I come out,' says England, 'when there are still raids and battles going on? If we were to leave, Egypt would be run over.' 'But there are no raids,' says the world. 'Oh, are there not?' says England, and then within a week sure enough the papers are full of some new raid of Dervishes. We are not all blind, Mister Headingly. We understand very well how such things can be done. A few Bedouins, a little backsheesh, some blank cartridges, and, behold—a raid!"

"Well, well," said the American, "I'm glad to know the rights of this business, for it has often puzzled me. But what does England get out of it?"

"She gets the country, monsieur."

"I see. You mean, for example, that there is a favourable tariff for British goods?"

"No, monsieur; it is the same for all."

"Well, then, she gives the contracts to Britishers?"

"Precisely, monsieur."

"For example, the railroad that they are building right through the country, the one that runs alongside the river, that would be a valuable contract for the British?"

Monsieur Fardet was an honest man, if an imaginative one.

"It is a French company, monsieur, which holds the railway contract," said he.

The American was puzzled.

"They don't seem to get much for their trouble," said he. "Still, of course, there must be some indirect pull somewhere. For example, Egypt no doubt has to pay and keepall those red-coats in Cairo."

"Egypt, monsieur! No, they are paid by England."

"Well, I suppose they know their ownbusiness best, but they seem to me to take a great deal of trouble, and to get mighty little in exchange. If they don't mind keeping order and guarding the frontier, with a constant war against the Dervishes on their hands, I don't know why any one should object. I suppose no one denies that the prosperity of the country has increased enormously since they came. The revenue returns show that. They tell me also that the poorer folks have justice, which they never had before."

"What are they doing here at all?" cried the Frenchman angrily. "Let them go back to their island. We cannot have them all over the world."

"Well, certainly, to us Americans, who live all in our own land, it does seem strange how you European nations are for ever slopping over into some other country which was not meant for you. It's easy for us to talk, of course, for we have still got room and to spare for all our people. When we begin pushing each other over the edge we shall have to start annexing also. But at present just here in North Africa there is Italy in Abyssinia, and England in Egypt, and France in Algiers—"

"France!" cried Monsieur Fardet. "Algiers belongs to France. You laugh, monsieur. I have the honour to wish you a very good-night." He rose from his seat, and walked off, rigid with outraged patriotism, to his cabin.

II

The young American hesitated for a little, debating in his mind whether he should not go down and post up the daily record of his impressions which he kept for his home-staying sister. But the cigars of Colonel Cochrane and of Cecil Brown were still twinkling in the far corner of the deck, and the student was acquisitive in the search of information. He did not quite know how to lead up to the matter, but the Colonel very soon did it for him.

"Come on, Headingly," said he, pushing a camp-stool in his direction. "This is the place for an antidote. I see that Fardet has been pouring politics into your ear."

"I can always recognise the confidential stoop of his shoulders when he discusses la haute politique," said the dandy diplomatist. "But what a sacrilege upon a night like this! What a nocturne in blue and silver might be suggested by that moon rising above the desert. There is a movement in one of Mendelssohn's songs which seems to embody it all—a sense of vastness, of repetition, the cry of the wind over an interminable expanse. The subtler emotions which cannot be translated into words are still to be hinted at by chords and harmonies."

"It seems wilder and more savage than ever to-night," remarked the American. "It gives me the same feeling of pitiless force that the Atlantic does upon a cold, dark, winter day. Perhaps it is the knowledge that we are right there on the very edge of any kind of law and order. How far do you suppose that we are from any Dervishes, Colonel Cochrane?"

"Well, on the Arabian side," said the Colonel, "we have the Egyptian fortified camp of Sarras about forty miles to the south of us. Beyond that are sixty miles of very wild country before you would come to the Dervish post at Akasheh. On this other side, however, there is nothing between us and them."

"Abousir is on this side, is it not?"

"Yes. That is why the excursion to the Abousir Rock has been forbidden for the last year. But things are quieter now."

"What is to prevent them from coming down on that side?"

"Absolutely nothing," said Cecil Brown, in his listless voice.

"Nothing, except their fears. The coming of course would be perfectly simple. The difficulty would lie in the return. They might find it hard to get back if their camels were spent, and the Halfa garrison with their beasts fresh got on their track. They know it as well as we do, and it has kept them from trying."

"It isn't safe to reckon upon a Dervish's fears," remarked Brown. "We must always bear in mind that they are not amenable to the same motives as other people. Many of them are anxious to meet death, and all of them are absolute, uncompromising believers in destiny. They exist as a reductio ad absurdum of all bigotry—a proof of how surely it leads towards blank barbarism."

"You think these people are a real menace to Egypt?" asked the American. "There seems from what I have heard to be some difference of opinion about it. Monsieur Fardet, for example, does not seem to think that the danger is a very pressing one."

"I am not a rich man," Colonel Cochrane answered after a little pause, "but I am prepared to lay all I am worth, that within three years of the British officers being withdrawn, the Dervishes would be upon the Mediterranean. Where would the civilisation of Egypt be? Where would the hundreds of millions which have been invested in this country? Where the monuments which all nations look upon as most precious memorials of the past?"

"Come now, Colonel," cried Headingly, laughing, "surely you don't mean that they would shift the pyramids?"

"You cannot foretell what they would do. There is no iconoclast in the world like an extreme Mohammedan. Last time they overran this country they burned the Alexandrian Library. You know that all representations of the human features are against the letter of the Koran. A statue is always an irreligious object in their eyes. What do these fellows care for the sentiment of Europe? The more they could offend it, the more delighted they would be. Down would go the Sphinx, the Colossi, the Statues of Abou-Simbel — as the saints went down in England before Cromwell's troopers."

"Well now," said Headingly, in his slow, thoughtful fashion, "suppose I grant you that the Dervishes could overrun Egypt, and suppose also that you English are holding them out, what I'm never done asking is, what reason have you for spending all these millions of dollars and the lives of so many of your men? What do you get out of it, more than France gets, or Germany, or any other country, that runs no risk and never lays out a cent?"

"There are a good many Englishmen who are asking themselves that question," remarked Cecil Brown. "It's my opinion that we have been the policemen of the world long enough. We policed the seas for pirates and slavers. Now we police the land for Dervishes and brigands and every sort of danger to civilisation. There is never a mad priest or a witch doctor, or a firebrand of any sort on this planet, who does not report his appearance by sniping the nearest British officer. One tires of it at last. If a Kurd breaks loose in Asia Minor, the world wants to know why Great Britain does not keep him in order. If there is a military mutiny in Egypt, or a Jehad in the Soudan, it is still Great Britain who has to set it right. And all to an accompaniment of curses such as the policeman gets when he seizes a ruffian among his pals. We get hard knocks and no thanks, and why should we do it? Let Europe do its own dirty work."

"Well," said Colonel Cochrane, crossing his legs and leaning forward with the decision of n man who has definite opinions, "I don't at all agree with you, Brown, and I think that to advocate such a course is to take a very limited view of our national duties. I think that behind national interests and diplomacy and all that there lies a great guiding force—a Providence, in fact—which is for ever getting the best out of each nation and using it for the good of the whole. When a nation ceases to respond, it is time that she went into hospital for a few centuries, like Spain or Greece—the virtue has gone out of her. A man or a nation is not placed upon this earth to do merely what is pleasant and what is profitable. It is often called upon to carry out what is both unpleasant and unprofitable, but if it is obviously right it is mere shirking not to undertake it."

Headingly nodded approvingly.

"Each has its own mission. Germany is predominant in abstract thought; France in literature, art, and grace. But we and you—for the English- speakers are all in the same boat, however much the New York Sun may scream over it—we and you have among our best men a higher conception of moral sense and public duty than is to be found in any other people. Now, these are the two qualities which are needed for directing a weaker race. You can't help them by abstract thought or by graceful art, but only by that moral sense which will hold the scales of Justice even, and keep itself free from every taint of corruption. That is how we rule India. We came there by a kind of natural law, like air rushing into a vacuum. All over the world, against our direct interests and our deliberate intentions, we are drawn into the same thing. And it will happen to you also. The pressure of destiny will force you to administer the Whole of America from Mexico to the Horn."

Headingly whistled.

"Our Jingoes would be pleased to hear you, Colonel Cochrane," said he. "They'd vote you into our Senate and make you one of the Committee on Foreign Relations."

"The world is small, and it grows smaller every day. It's a single organic body, and one spot of gangrene is enough to vitiate the whole. There's no room upon it for dishonest, defaulting, tyrannical, irresponsible Governments. As long as they exist they will always be sources of trouble and of danger. But there are many races which appear to be so incapable of improvement that we can never hope to get a good Government out of them. What is to be done, then? The former device of Providence in such a case was extermination by some more virile stock—an Attila or a Tamerlane pruned off the weaker branch. Now, we have a more merciful substitution of rulers, or even of mere advice from a more advanced race.

That is the case with the Central Asian Khanates and with the protected States of India. If the work has to be done, and if we are the best fitted for the work, then I think that it would be a cowardice and a crime to shirk it."

"But who is to decide whether it is a fitting case for your interference?" objected the American. "A predatory country could grab every other land in the world upon such a pretext."

"Events—inexorable, inevitable events—will decide it. Take this Egyptian business as an example. In 1881 there was nothing in this world further from the minds of our people than any interference with Egypt; and yet 1882 left us in possession of the country. There was never any choice in the chain of events. A massacre in the streets of Alexandria, and the mounting of guns to drive out our fleet—which was there, you understand, in fulfilment of solemn treaty obligations—led to the bombardment. The bombardment led to a landing to save the city from destruction. The landing caused an extension of operations—and here we are, with the country upon our hands. At the time of trouble we begged and implored the French, or any one else, to come and help us to put the thing to rights, but they all deserted us when there was work to be done, although they are ready enough to scold and to impede us now. When we tried to get out of it, up came this wild Dervish movement, and we had to sit tighter than ever. We never wanted the task; but, now that it has come, we must put it through in a workmanlike manner. We've brought justice into the country, and purity of administration, and protection for the poor man. It has made more advance in the last twelve years than since the Moslem invasion in the seventh century. Except the pay of a couple of hundred men, who spend their money in the country, England has neither directly nor indirectly made a shilling out of it, and I don't believe you will find in history a more successful and more disinterested bit of work."

Headingly puffed thoughtfully at his cigarette.

"There is a house near ours, down on the Back Bay at Boston, which just ruins the whole prospect," said he. "It has old chairs littered about the stoop, and the shingles are loose, and the garden runs wild; but I don't know that the neighbours are exactly justified in rushing in, and stamping around, and running the thing on their own lines."

"Not if it were on fire?" asked the Colonel.

Headingly laughed, and rose from his camp-stool.

"Well, it doesn't come within the provisions of the Monroe Doctrine, Colonel," said he. "I'm beginning to realise that modern Egypt is every bit as interesting as ancient, and that Rameses the Second wasn't the last live man in the country."

The two Englishmen rose and yawned.

"Yes, it's a whimsical freak of fortune which has sent men from a little island in the Atlantic to administer the land of the Pharaohs," remarked

Cecil Brown. "We shall pass away again, and never leave a trace among these successive races who have held the country, for it is not an Anglo-Saxon custom to write their deeds upon rocks. I dare say that the remains of a Cairo drainage system will be our most permanent record, unless they prove a thousand years hence that it was the work of the Hyksos kings. But here is the shore party come back."

Down below they could hear the mellow Irish accents of Mrs. Belmont and the deep voice of her husband, the iron-grey rifle-shot. Mr. Stuart, the fat Birmingham clergyman, was thrashing out a question of piastres with a noisy donkey-boy, and the others were joining in with chaff and advice. Then the hubbub died away, the party from above came down the ladder, there were "good-nights," the shutting of doors, and the little steamer lay silent, dark, and motionless in the shadow of the high Halfa bank. And beyond this one point of civilisation and of comfort there lay the limitless, savage, unchangeable desert, straw-coloured and dream-like in the moonlight, mottled over with the black shadows of the hills.

III

"Stoppa! Backa!" cried the native pilot to the European engineer.

The bluff bows of the stern-wheeler had squelched into the soft brown mud, and the current had swept the boat alongside the bank. The long gangway was thrown across, and the six tall soldiers of the Soudanese escort filed along it, their light-blue gold-trimmed zouave uniforms, and their jaunty yellow and red forage-caps, showing up bravely in the clear morning light. Above them, on the top of the bank, was ranged the line of donkeys, and the air was full of the clamour of the boys. In shrill strident voices each was crying out the virtues of his own beast, and abusing that of his neighbour.

Colonel Cochrane and Mr. Belmont stood together in the bows, each wearing the broad white puggareed hat of the tourist. Miss Adams and her niece leaned against the rail beside them.

"Sorry your wife isn't coming, Belmont," said the Colonel.

"I think she had a touch of the sun yesterday. Her head aches very badly. "

His voice was strong and thick like his figure.

"I should stay to keep her company, Mr. Belmont," said the little American old maid; "but I learn that Mrs. Shlesinger finds the ride too long for her, and has some letters which she must mail to-day, so Mrs. Belmont will not be lonesome."

"You're very good, Miss Adams. We shall be back, you know, by two o'clock."

"Is that certain?"

"It must be certain, for we are taking no lunch with us, and we shall be famished by then."

"Yes, I expect we shall be ready for a hock and seltzer at any rate," said the Colonel. "This desert dust gives a flavour to the worst wine."

"Now, ladies and gentlemen!" cried Mansoor, the dragoman, moving forward with something of the priest in his flowing garments and smooth, clean-shaven face. "We must start early that we may return before the meridial heat of the weather. "He ran his dark eyes over the little group of his tourists with a paternal expression. "You take your green glasses, Miss Adams, for glare very great out in the desert. Ah, Mr. Stuart, I set aside very fine donkey for you —prize donkey, sir, always put aside for the gentleman of most weight. Never mind to take your monument ticket to-day. Now, ladies and gentlemen, if you please!"

Like a grotesque frieze the party moved one by one along the plank gangway and up the brown crumbling bank. Mr. Stephens led them, a thin, dry, serious figure, in an English straw hat. His red "Baedeker" gleamed under his arm, and in one hand he held a little paper of notes, as if it were a brief. He took Miss Sadie by one arm and her aunt by the other as they toiled up the bank, and the young girl's laughter rang frank and clear in the morning air as "Baedeker" came fluttering down at their feet. Mr. Belmont and Colonel Cochrane followed, the brims of their sun-hats touching as they discussed the relative advantages of the Mauser, the Lebel, and the Lee-Metford. Behind them walked Cecil Brown, listless, cynical, self-contained. The fat clergyman puffed slowly up the bank, with many gasping witticisms at his own defects. "I'm one of those men who carry everything before them," said he, glancing ruefully at his rotundity, and chuckling wheezily at his own little joke. Last of all came Headingly, slight and tall, with the student stoop about his shoulders, and Fardet, the good-natured, fussy, argumentative Parisian.

"You see we have an escort to-day," he whispered to his companion.

"So I observed."

"Pah!" cried the Frenchman, throwing out his arms in derision; "as well have an escort from Paris to Versailles. This is all part of the play, Monsieur Headingly. It deceives no one, but it is part of the play. Pourquoi ces droles de militaires, dragoman, hein?"

It was the dragoman's role to be all things to all men, so he looked cautiously round before he answered, to make sure that the English were mounted and out of earshot.

"C'est ridicule, monsieur!" said he, shrugging his fat shoulders. "Mais que voulez-vous? C'est l'ordre official Egyptien. "

"Egyptien! Pah, Anglais, Anglais—toujours Anglais!" cried the angry Frenchman.

The frieze now was more grotesque than ever, but had changed suddenly to an equestrian one, sharply outlined against the deep-blue Egyptian sky. Those who have never ridden before have to ride in Egypt, and when the donkeys break into a canter, and the Nile Irregulars are at full charge, such a scene of flying veils, clutching hands, huddled swaying figures, and anxious faces is nowhere to be seen. Belmont, his square figure balanced upon a small white donkey, was waving his hat to his wife, who had come out upon the saloon-deck of the Korosko. Cochrane sat very erect with a stiff military seat, hands low, head high, and heels down, while beside him rode the young Oxford man, looking about him with drooping eyelids as if he thought the desert hardly respectable, and had his doubts about the Universe. Behind them the whole party was strung along the bank in varying stages of jolting and discomfort, a brown-faced, noisy donkey-boy running after each donkey. Looking back, they could see the little lead-coloured stern-wheeler, with the gleam of Mrs. Belmont's handkerchief from the deck. Beyond ran the broad, brown river, winding down in long curves to where, five miles off, the square, white block-houses upon the black, ragged hills marked the outskirts of Wady Halfa, which had been their starting-point that morning.

"Isn't it just too lovely for anything?" cried Sadie joyously. "I've got a donkey that runs on casters, and the saddle is just elegant. Did you ever see anything so cunning as these beads and things round his neck? You must make a memo. re donkey, Mr. Stephens. Isn't that correct legal English?"

Stephens looked at the pretty, animated, boyish face looking up at him from under the coquettish straw hat, and he wished that he had the courage to tell her in her own language that she was just too sweet for anything. But he feared above all things lest he should offend her, and so put an end to their present pleasant intimacy. So his compliment dwindled into a smile.

"You look very happy," said he.

"Well, who could help feeling good with this dry, clear air, and the blue sky, and the crisp yellow sand, and a superb donkey to carry you? I've just got everything in the world to make me happy."

"Everything?"

"Well, everything I have any use for just now."

"I suppose you never know what it is to be sad?"

"Oh, when I am miserable, I am just too miserable for words. I've sat and cried for days and days at Smith's College, and the other girls were just crazy to know what I was crying about, and guessing what the reason was that I wouldn't tell them, when all the time the real true reason was that I didn't know myself. You know how it comes like a great dark shadow over you, and you don't know why or wherefore, but you've just got to settle down to it and be miserable."

"But you never had any real cause?"

"No, Mr. Stephens, I've had such a good time all my life that I really don't think, when I look back, that I ever had any real cause for sorrow."

"Well, Miss Sadie, I hope with all my heart that you will be able to say the same when you are the same age as your aunt. Surely I hear her calling."

"I wish, Mr. Stephens, you would strike my donkey-boy with your whip if he hits the donkey again," cried Miss Adams, jogging up on a high, raw-boned beast. "Hi, dragoman, Mansoor, you tell this boy that I won't have the animals ill used, and that he ought to be ashamed of himself. Yes, you little rascal, you ought! He's grinning at me like an advertisement for a tooth paste. Do you think, Mr. Stephens, that if I were to knit that black soldier a pair of woollen stockings he would be allowed to wear them? The poor creature has bandages round his legs."

"Those are his putties, Miss Adams," said Colonel Cochrane, looking back at her. "We have found in India that they are the best support to the leg in marching. They are very much better than any stocking."

"Well, you don't say! They remind me mostly of a sick horse. But it's elegant to have the soldiers with us, though Monsieur Fardet tells me there's nothing for us to be scared about."

"That is only my opinion, Miss Adams," said the Frenchman hastily. "It may be that Colonel Cochrane thinks otherwise."

"It is Monsieur Fardet's opinion against that of the officers who have the responsibility of caring for the safety of the frontier," said the Colonel coldly. "At least we will all agree that they have the effect of making the scene very much more picturesque."

The desert upon their right lay in long curves of sand, like the dunes which might have fringed some forgotten primeval sea. Topping them they could see the black, craggy summits of the curious volcanic hills which rise upon the Libyan side. On the crest of the low sand-hills they would catch a glimpse every now and then of a tall, sky-blue soldier, walking swiftly, his rifle at the trail. For a moment the lank, warlike figure would be sharply silhouetted against the sky. Then he would dip into a hollow and disappear, while some hundred yards off another would show for an instant and vanish.

"Wherever are they raised?" asked Sadie, watching the moving figures. "They look to me just about the same tint as the hotel boys in the States."

"I thought some question might arise about them," said Mr. Stephens, who was never so happy as when he could anticipate some wish of the pretty American. "I made one or two references this morning in the ship's library. Here it is—re—that's to say, about black soldiers. I have it on my notes that they are from the 10th Soudanese battalion of the Egyptian army. They are recruited from the Dinkas and the Shilluks— two negroid tribes living to the south of the Dervish country, near the Equator. "

"How can the recruits come through the Dervishes, then?" asked Headingly sharply.

"I dare say there is no such very great difficulty over that," said Monsieur Fardet, with a wink at the American.

"The older men are the remains of the old black battalions. Some of them served with Gordon at Khartoum, and have his medal to show. The others are many of them deserters from the Mahdi's army," said the Colonel.

"Well, so long as they are not wanted, they look right elegant in those blue jackets," Miss Adams observed. "But if there was any trouble, I guess we would wish they were less ornamental and a bit whiter."

"I am not so sure of that, Miss Adams," said the Colonel. "I have seen these fellows in the field, and I assure you that I have the utmost confidence in their steadiness."

"Well, I'll take your word without trying," said Miss Adams, with a decision which made every one smile.

So far their road had lain along the side of the river, which was swirling down upon their left hand deep and strong from the cataracts above. Here and there the rush of the current was broken by a black shining boulder over which the foam was spouting. Higher up they could see the white gleam of the rapids, and the banks grew into rugged cliffs, which were capped by a peculiar, outstanding semi-circular rock. It did not require the dragoman's aid to tell the party that this was the famous landmark to which they were bound. A long, level stretch lay before them, and the donkeys took it at a canter. At the farther side were scattered rocks, black upon orange;and in the midst of them rose some broken shafts of pillars and a length of engraved wall, looking in its greyness and its solidity more like some work of Nature than of man. The fat, sleek dragoman had dismounted, and stood waiting in his petticoats and his cover-coat for the stragglers to gather round him.

"This temple, ladies and gentlemen," he cried, with the air of an auctioneer who is about to sell it to the highest bidder, "very fine example from the eighteenth dynasty. Here is the cartouche of Thotmes the Third," he pointed up with his donkey-whip at the rude, but deep, hieroglyphics upon the wall above him. "He live sixteen hundred years before Christ, and this is made to remember his victorious exhibition into Mesopotamia. Here we have his history from the time that he was with his mother, until he return with captives tied to his chariot. In this you see him crowned with Lower Egypt, and with Upper Egypt offering up sacrifice in honour of his victory to the God Ammon-ra. Here he bring his captives before him, and he cut off each his right hand. In this corner you see little pile—all right hands."

"My sakes, I shouldn't have liked to be here in those days," said Miss Adams.

"Why, there's nothing altered," remarked Cecil Brown. "The East is still the East. I've no doubt that within a hundred miles, or perhaps a good deal less, from where you stand—"

"Shut up!" whispered the Colonel, and the party shuffled on down the line of the wall with their faces up and their big hats thrown backwards. The sun behind them struck the old grey masonry with a brassy glare, and carried on to it the strange black shadows of the tourists, mixing them up with the grim, high-nosed, square-shouldered warriors, and the grotesque, rigid deities who lined it. The broad shadow of the Reverend John Stuart, of Birmingham, smudged out both the heathen King and the god whom he worshipped.

"What's this?" he was asking in his wheezy voice, pointing up with a yellow Assouan cane.

"That is a hippopotamus," said the dragoman; and the tourists all tittered, for there was just a suspicion of Mr. Stuart himself in the carving.

"But it isn't bigger than a little pig," he protested. "You see that the King is putting his spear through it with ease."

"They make it small to show that it was a very small thing to the King," said the dragoman. "So you see that all the King's prisoners do not exceed his knee—which is not because he was so much taller, but so much more powerful. You see that he is bigger than his horse, because he is a king and the other is only a horse. The same way, these small women whom you see here and there are just his trivial little wives."

"Well, now!" cried Miss Adams indignantly. "If they had sculpted that King's soul it would have needed a lens to see it. Fancy his allowing his wives to be put in like that."

"If he did it now, Miss Adams," said the Frenchman, "he would have more fighting than ever in Mesopotamia. But time brings revenge. Perhaps the day will soon come when we have the picture of the big strong wife and the trivial little husband—hein?"

Cecil Brown and Headingly had dropped behind, for the glib comments of the dragoman, and the empty, light-hearted chatter of the tourists jarred upon their sense of solemnity. They stood in silence watching the grotesque procession, with its sun-hats and green veils, as it passed in the vivid sunshine down the front of the old grey wall. Above them two crested hoopoes were fluttering and calling amid the ruins of the pylon.

"Isn't it a sacrilege?" said the Oxford man at last.

"Well, now, I'm glad you feel that about it, because it's how it always strikes me," Headingly answered with feeling. "I'm not quite clear in my own mind how these things should be approached—if they are to be approached at all—but I am sure this is not the way. On the whole, I prefer the ruins that I have not seen to those which I have."

The young diplomatist looked up with his peculiarly bright smile, which faded away too soon into his languid, blase mask.

"I've got a map," said the American, "and sometimes far away from anything in the very midst of the waterless, trackless desert, I see 'ruins' marked upon it—or 'remains of a temple,' perhaps. For example, the temple of Jupiter Ammon, which was one of the most considerable shrines in the world, was hundreds of miles away back of anywhere. Those are the ruins, solitary, unseen, unchanging through the centuries, which appeal to one's imagination. But when I present a check at the door, and go in as if it were Barnum's show, all the subtle feeling of romance goes right out of it."

"Absolutely!" said Cecil Brown, looking over the desert with his dark, intolerant eyes. "If one could come wandering here alone—stumble upon it by chance, as it were—and find one's self in absolute solitude in the dim light of the temple, with these grotesque figures all round, it would be perfectly overwhelming. A man would be prostrated with wonder and awe. But when Belmont is puffing his bulldog pipe, and Stuart is wheezing, and Miss Sadie Adams is laughing—"

"And that jay of a dragoman speaking his piece," said Headingly; "I want to stand and think all the time, and I never seem to get the chance. I was ripe for manslaughter when I stood before the Great Pyramid, and couldn't get a quiet moment because they would boost me on to the top. I took a kick at one man which would have sent him to the top in one jump if I had hit meat. But fancy travelling all the way from America to see the pyramid, and then finding nothing better to do than to kick an Arab in front of it!"

The Oxford man laughed in his gentle, tired fashion. "They are starting again," said he, and the two hastened forwards to take their places at the tail of the absurd procession.

Their route ran now among large, scattered boulders, and between stony, shingly hills. A narrow winding path curved in and out amongst the rocks. Behind them their view was cut off by similar hills, black and fantastic, like the slag-heaps at the shaft of a mine. A silence fell upon the little company, and even Sadie's bright face reflected the harshness of Nature. The escort had closed in, and marched beside them, their boots scrunching among the loose black rubble. Colonel Cochrane and Belmont were still riding together in the van.

"Do you know, Belmont," said the Colonel, in a low voice, "you may think me a fool, but I don't like this one little bit."

Belmont gave a short gruff laugh.

"It seemed all right in the saloon of the Korosko, but now that we are here we do seem rather up in the air," said he. "Still, you know, a party comes here every week, and nothing has ever gone wrong."

"I don't mind taking my chances when I am on the war-path," the Colonel answered. "That's all straightforward and in the way of business. But when you have women with you, and a helpless crowd like this, it becomes really dreadful. Of course, the chances are a hundred to one that we have no trouble; but if we should have—well, it won't bear thinking about. The wonderful thing is their complete unconsciousness that there is any danger whatever."

"Well, I like the English tailor-made dresses well enough for walking, Mr. Stephens," said Miss Sadie from behind them. "But for an afternoon dress, I think the French have more style than the English. Your milliners have a more severe cut, and they don't do the cunning little ribbons and bows and things in the same way."

The Colonel smiled at Belmont.

"She is quite serene in her mind, at any rate," said he. "Of course, I wouldn't say what I think to any one but you, and I daresay it will all prove to be quite unfounded."

"Well, I could imagine parties of Dervishes on the prowl," said Belmont. "But what I cannot imagine is that they should just happen to come to the pulpit rock on the very morning when we are due there."

"Considering that our movements have been freely advertised, and that every one knows a week beforehand what our programme is, and where we are to be found, it does not strike me as being such a wonderful coincidence."

"It is a very remote chance," said Belmont stoutly, but he was glad in his heart that his wife was safe and snug on board the steamer.

And now they were clear of the rocks again, with a fine stretch of firm yellow sand extending to the very base of the conical hill which lay before them. "Ay-ah! Ay-ah!" cried the boys, whack came their sticks upon the flanks of the donkeys, which broke into a gallop, and away they all streamed over the plain. It was not until they had come to the end of the path which curves up the hill that the dragoman called a halt.

"Now, ladies and gentlemen, we are arrived for the so famous pulpit rock of Abousir. From the summit you will presently enjoy a panorama of remarkable fertility. But first you will observe that over the rocky side of the hill are everywhere cut the names of great men who have passed it in their travels, and some of these names are older than the time of Christ."

"Got Moses?" asked Miss Adams.

"Auntie, I'm surprised at you!" cried Sadie.

"Well, my dear, he was in Egypt, and he was a great man, and he may have passed this way."

"Moses's name very likely there, and the same with Herodotus," said the dragoman gravely. "Both have been long worn away. But there on the brown rock you will see Belzoni. And up higher is Gordon. There is hardly a name famous in the Soudan which you will not find, if you like. And now, with your permission, we shall take good-bye of our donkeys and walk up the path, and you will see the river and the desert from the summit of the top."

A minute or two of climbing brought them out upon the semicircular platform which crowns the rock. Below them on the far side was a perpendicular black cliff, a hundred and fifty feet high, with the swirling, foam-streaked river roaring past its base. The swish of the water and the low roar as it surged over the mid-stream boulders boomed through the hot, stagnant air. Far up and far down they could see the course of the river, a quarter of a mile in breadth, and running very deep and strong, with sleek black eddies and occasional spoutings of foam. On the other side was a frightful wilderness of black, scattered rocks, which were the debris carried down by the river at high flood. In no direction were there any signs of human beings or their dwellings.

"On the far side," said the dragoman, waving his donkey-whip towards the east, "is the military line which conducts Wady Halfa to Sarras. Sarras lies to the south, under that black hill. Those two blue mountains which you see very far away are in Dongola, more than a hundred miles from Sarras. The railway there is forty miles long, and has been much annoyed by the Dervishes, who are very glad to turn the rails into spears. The telegraph wires are also much appreciated thereby. Now, if you will kindly turn round, I will explain, also, what we see upon the other side."

It was a view which, when once seen, must always haunt the mind. Such an expanse of savage and unrelieved desert might be part of some cold and burned-out planet rather than of this fertile and bountiful earth. Away and away it stretched to die into a soft, violet haze in the extremest distance. In the foreground the sand was of a bright golden yellow, which was quite dazzling in the sunshine. Here and there, in a scattered cordon, stood the six trusty negro soldiers leaning motionless upon their rifles, and each throwing a shadow which looked as solid as himself. But beyond this golden plain lay a low line of those black slag-heaps, with yellow sand-valleys winding between them. These in their turn were topped by higher and more fantastic hills, and these by others, peeping over each other's shoulders until they blended with that distant violet haze. None of these hills were of any height—a few hundred feet at the most—but their savage, saw-toothed crests, and their steep scarps of sun-baked stone, gave them a fierce character of their own.

"The Libyan Desert," said the dragoman, with a proud wave of his hand. "The greatest desert in the world. Suppose you travel right west from here, and turn neither to the north nor to the south, the first houses you would come to would be in America. That make you home-sick, Miss Adams, I believe?"

But the American old maid had her attention drawn away by the conduct of Sadie, who had caught her arm by one hand and was pointing over the desert with the other.

"Well, now, if that isn't too picturesque for anything!" she cried, with a flush of excitement upon her pretty face. "Do look, Mr. Stephens! That's just the one only thing we wanted to make it just perfectly grand. See the men upon the camels coming out from between those hills!"

They all looked at the long string of red-turbaned riders who were winding out of the ravine, and there fell such a hush that the buzzing of the flies sounded quite loud upon their ears. Colonel Cochrane had lit a match, and he stood with it in one hand and the unlit cigarette in the other until the flame licked round his fingers. Belmont whistled. The dragoman stood staring with his mouth half-open, and a curious slaty tint in his full, red lips. The others looked from one to the other with an uneasy sense that there was something wrong. It was the Colonel who broke the silence.

"By George, Belmont, I believe the hundred-to-one chance has come off!" said he.

IV

"What's the meaning of this, Mansoor?" cried Belmont harshly. "Who are these people, and why are you standing staring as if you had lost your senses?"

The dragoman made an effort to compose himself, and licked his dry lips before he answered.

"I do not know who they are," said he in a quavering voice.

"Who they are?" cried the Frenchman. "You can see who they are. They are armed men upon camels, Ababdeh, Bishareen—Bedouins, in short, such as are employed by the Government upon the frontier."

"Be Jove, he may be right, Cochrane," said Belmont, looking inquiringly at the Colonel. "Why shouldn't it be as he says? why shouldn't these fellows be friendlies?"

"There are no friendlies upon this side of the river," said the Colonel abruptly; "I am perfectly certain about that. There is no use in mincing matters. We must prepare for the worst."

But in spite of his words, they stood stock-still, in a huddled group, staring out over the plain. Their nerves were numbed by the sudden shock, and to all of them it was like a scene in a dream, vague, impersonal, and unreal. The men upon the camels had streamed out from a gorge which lay a mile or so distant on the side of the path along which they had travelled. Their retreat, therefore, was entirely cut off. It appeared, from the dust and the length of the line, to be quite an army which was emerging from the hills, for seventy men upon camels cover a considerable stretch of ground. Having reached the sandy plain, they very deliberately formed to the front, and then at the harsh call of a bugle they trotted forward in line, the parti-coloured figures all swaying and the sand smoking in a rolling yellow cloud at the heels of their camels. At the same moment the six black soldiers doubled in from the front with their Martinis at the trail, and snuggled down like well-trained skirmishers behind the rocks upon the haunch of the hill. Their breech blocks all snapped together as their corporal gave them the order to load.

And now suddenly the first stupor of the excursionists passed away, and was succeeded by a frantic and impotent energy. They all ran about upon the plateau of rock in an aimless, foolish flurry, like frightened fowls in a yard. They could not bring themselves to acknowledge that there was no possible escape for them. Again and again they rushed to the edge of the great cliff which rose from the river, but the youngest and most daring of them could never have descended it. The two women clung one on each side of the trembling Mansoor, with a feeling that he was officially responsible for their safety. When he ran up and down in his desperation, his skirts and theirs all fluttered together. Stephens, the lawyer, kept close to Sadie Adams, muttering mechanically, "Don't be alarmed, Miss Sadie; don't be at all alarmed!" though his own limbs were twitching with agitation. Monsieur Fardet stamped about with a guttural rolling of r's, glancing angrily at his companions as if they had in some way betrayed him; while the fat clergyman stood with his umbrella up, staring stolidly with big, frightened eyes at the camel-men. Cecil Brown curled his small, prim moustache, and looked white, but contemptuous. The Colonel, Belmont, and the young Harvard graduate were the three most cool-headed and resourceful members of the party.

"Better stick together," said the Colonel. "There's no escape for us, so we may as well remain united."

"They've halted," said Belmont.

"They are reconnoitring us. They know very well that there is no escape from them, and they are taking their time. I don't see what we can do."

"Suppose we hide the women," Headingly suggested. "They can't know how many of us are here. When they have taken us, the women can come out of their hiding-place and make their way back to the boat."

"Admirable!" cried Colonel Cochrane. "Admirable! This way, please, Miss Adams. Bring the ladies here, Mansoor. There is not an instant to be lost."

There was a part of the plateau which was invisible from the plain, and here in feverish haste they built a little cairn. Many flaky slabs of stone were lying about, and it did not take long to prop the largest of these against a rock, so as to make a lean-to, and then to put two side-pieces to complete it. The slabs were of the same colour as the rock, so that to a casual glance the hiding-place was not very visible. The two ladies were squeezed into this, and they crouched together, Sadie's arms thrown round her aunt. When they had walled them up, the men turned with lighter hearts to see what was going on. As they did so there rang out the sharp, peremptory crack of a rifle-shot from the escort, followed by another and another, but these isolated shots were drowned in the long, spattering roll of an irregular volley from the plain, and the air was full of the phit-phit-phit of the bullets. The tourists all huddled behind the rocks, with the exception of the Frenchman, who still stamped angrily about, striking his sun-hat with his clenched hand. Belmont and Cochrane crawled down to where the Soudanese soldiers were firing slowly and steadily, resting their rifles upon the boulders in front of them.

The Arabs had halted about five hundred yards away, and it was evident from their leisurely movements that they were perfectly aware that there was no possible escape for the travellers. They had paused to ascertain their number before closing in upon them. Most of them were firing from the backs of their camels, but a few had dismounted and were kneeling here and there —little shimmering white spots against the golden back-ground. Their shots came sometimes singly in quick, sharp throbs, and sometimes in a rolling volley, with a sound like a boy's stick drawn across iron railings. The hill buzzed like a bee-hive, and the bullets made a sharp crackling as they struck against the rocks.

"You do no good by exposing yourself," said Belmont, drawing Colonel Cochrane behind a large jagged boulder, which already furnished a shelter for three of the Soudanese. "A bullet is the best we have to hope for," said Cochrane grimly. "What an infernal fool I have been, Belmont, not to protest more energetically against this ridiculous expedition! I deserve whatever I get, but it is hard on these poor souls who never knew the danger."

"I suppose there's no help for us?"

"Not the faintest."

"Don't you think this firing might bring the troops up from Halfa?"

"They'll never hear it. It is a good six miles from here to the steamer. From that to Halfa would be another five."

"Well, when we don't return, the steamer will give the alarm."

"And where shall we be by that time?"

"My poor Norah! My poor little Norah!" muttered Belmont, in the depths of his grizzled moustache.

"What do you suppose that they will do with us, Cochrane?" he asked after a pause.

"They may cut our throats, or they may take us as slaves to Khartoum. I don't know that there is much to choose. There's one of us out of his troubles anyhow."

The soldier next them had sat down abruptly, and leaned forward over his knees. His movement and attitude were so natural that it was hard to realise that he had been shot through the head. He neither stirred nor groaned. His comrades bent over him for a moment, and then, shrugging their shoulders, they turned their dark faces to the Arabs once more. Belmont picked up the dead man's Martini and his ammunition-pouch.

"Only three more rounds, Cochrane," said he, with the little brass cylinders upon the palm of his hand. "We've let them shoot too soon, and too often. We should have waited for the rush."

"You're a famous shot, Belmont," cried the Colonel. "I've heard of you as one of the cracks. Don't you think you could pick off their leader?"

"Which is he?"

"As far as I can make out, it is that one on the white camel on their right front. I mean the fellow who is peering at us from under his two hands. "

Belmont thrust in his cartridge and altered the sights. "It's a shocking bad light for judging distance," said he. "This is where the low point-blank trajectory of the Lee-Metford comes in useful. Well, we'll try him at five hundred." He fired, but there was no change in the white camel or the peering rider.

"Did you see any sand fly?"

"No, I saw nothing."

"I fancy I took my sight a trifle too full."

"Try him again."

Man and rifle and rock were equally steady, but again the camel and chief remained un-harmed. The third shot must have been nearer, for he moved a few paces to the right, as if he were becoming restless. Belmont threw the empty rifle down, with an exclamation of disgust.

"It's this confounded light," he cried, and his cheeks flushed with annoyance. "Think of my wasting three cartridges in that fashion! If I had him at Bisley I'd shoot the turban off him, but this vibrating glare means refraction. What's the matter with the Frenchman?"

Monsieur Fardet was stamping about the plateau with the gestures of a man who has been stung by a wasp. "S'cré nom! S'cré nom!" he shouted, showing his strong white teeth under his black waxed moustache. He wrung his right hand violently, and as he did so he sent a little spray of blood from his finger-tips. A bullet had chipped his wrist. Headingly ran out from the cover where be had been crouching, with the intention of dragging the demented Frenchman into a place of safety, but he had not taken three paces before he was himself hit in the loins, and fell with a dreadful crash among the stones. He staggered to his feet, and then fell again in the same place, floundering up and down like a horse which has broken its back.

"I'm done!" he whispered, as the Colonel ran to his aid, and then he lay still, with his china-white cheek against the black stones. When, but a year before, he had wandered under the elms of Cambridge, surely the last fate upon this earth which he could have predicted for himself would be that he should be slain by the bullet of a fanatical Mohammedan in the wilds of the Libyan Desert.

Meanwhile the fire of the escort had ceased, for they had shot away their last cartridge. A second man had been killed, and a third—who was the corporal in charge—had received a bullet in his thigh. He sat upon a stone, tying up his injury with a grave, preoccupied look upon his wrinkled black face, like an old woman piecing together a broken plate. The three others fastened their bayonets with a determined metallic rasp and snap, and the air of men who intended to sell their lives dearly.

"They're coming!" cried Belmont, looking over the plain.

"Let them come!" the Colonel answered, putting his hands into his trouser- pockets. Suddenly he pulled one fist out, and shook it furiously in the air. "Oh, the cads! the confounded cads!" he shouted, and his eyes were congested with rage.

It was the fate of the poor donkey-boys which had carried the self-contained soldier out of his usual calm. During the firing they had remained huddled, a pitiable group, among the rocks at the base of the hill. Now upon the conviction that the charge of the Dervishes must come first upon them, they had sprung upon their animals with shrill, inarticulate cries of fear, and had galloped off across the plain. A small flanking-party of eight or ten camel-men had worked round while the firing had been going on, and these dashed in among the flying donkey-boys, hacking and hewing with a cold-blooded, deliberate ferocity. One little boy, in a flapping Galabeeah, kept ahead of his pursuers for a time, but the long stride of the camels ran him down, and an Arab thrust his spear into the middle of his stooping back. The small, white-clad corpses looked like a flock of sheep trailing over the desert.

But the people upon the rock had no time to think of the cruel fate of the donkey-boys. Even the Colonel, after that first indignant outburst, had forgotten all about them. The advancing camel-men had trotted to the bottom of the hill, had dismounted, and leaving their camels kneeling, had rushed furiously onward. Fifty of them were clambering up the path and over the rocks together, their red turbans appearing and vanishing again as they scrambled over the boulders. Without a shot or a pause they surged over the three black soldiers, killing one and stamping the other two down under their hurrying feet. So they burst on to the plateau at the top, where an unexpected resistance checked them for an instant.

The travellers, nestling up against one another, had awaited, each after his own fashion, the coming of the Arabs. The Colonel, with his hands back in his trouser-pockets, tried to whistle out of his dry lips. Belmont folded his arms and leaned against a rock, with a sulky frown upon his lowering face. So strangely do our minds act that his three successive misses, and the tarnish to his reputation as a marksman, was troubling him more than his impending fate. Cecil Brown stood erect, and plucked nervously at the up-turned points of his little prim moustache. Monsieur Fardet groaned over his wounded wrist. Mr. Stephens, in sombre impotence, shook his head slowly, the living embodiment of prosaic law and order. Mr. Stuart stood, his umbrella still over him, with no expression upon his heavy face, or in his staring brown eyes. Headingly lay with that china-white cheek resting motionless upon the stones. His sun-hat had fallen off, and he looked quite boyish with his ruffled yellow hair and his un-lined, clean-cut face. The dragoman sat upon a stone and played nervously with his donkey-whip. So the Arabs found them when they reached the summit of the hill.

And then, just as the foremost rushed to lay hands upon them, a most unexpected incident arrested them. From the time of the first appearance of the Dervishes the fat clergyman of Birmingham had looked like a man in a cataleptic trance. He had neither moved nor spoken. But now he suddenly woke at a bound into strenuous and heroic energy. It may have been the mania of fear, or it may have been the blood of some Berserk ancestor which stirred suddenly in his veins; but he broke into a wild shout, and, catching up a stick, he struck right and left among the Arabs with a fury which was more savage than their own. One who helped to draw up this narrative has left it upon record that, of all the pictures which have been burned into his brain, there is none so clear as that of this man, his large face shining with perspiration, and his great body dancing about with unwieldy agility, as he struck at the shrinking, snarling savages.

Then a spear-head flashed from behind a rock with a quick, vicious, upward thrust, the clergyman fell upon his hands and knees, and the horde poured over him to seize their unresisting victims. Knives glimmered before their eyes, rude hands clutched at their wrists and at their throats, and then, with brutal and unreasoning violence, they were hauled and pushed down the steep winding path to where the camels were waiting below. The Frenchman waved his unwounded hand as he walked. "Vive le Khalifa! Vive le Madhi!" he shouted, until a blow from behind with the butt-end of a Remington beat him into silence.

And now they were herded in at the base of the Abousir rock, this little group of modern types who had fallen into the rough clutch of the seventh century—for in all save the rifles in their hands there was nothing to distinguish these men from the desert warriors who first carried the crescent flag out of Arabia. The East does not change, and the Dervish raiders were not less brave, less cruel, or less fanatical than their forebears. They stood in a circle, leaning upon their guns and spears, and looking with exultant eyes at the dishevelled group of captives. They were clad in some approach to a uniform, red turbans gathered around the neck as well as the head, so that the fierce face looked out of a scarlet frame; yellow, untanned shoes, and white tunics with square brown patches let into them. All carried rifles, and one had a small discoloured bugle slung over his shoulder. Half of them were negroes—fine, muscular men, with the limbs of a jet Hercules; and the other half were Baggara Arabs—small, brown, and wiry, with little, vicious eyes, and thin, cruel lips. The chief was also a Baggara, but he was a taller man than the others, with a black beard which came down over his chest, and a pair of hard, cold eyes, which gleamed like glass from under his thick, black brows. They were fixed now upon his captives, and his features were grave with thought. Mr. Stuart had been brought down, his hat gone, his face still flushed with anger, and his trousers sticking in one part to his leg. The two surviving Soudanese soldiers, their black faces and blue coats blotched with crimson, stood silently at attention upon one side of this forlorn group of castaways.

The chief stood for some minutes, stroking his black beard, while his fierce eyes glanced from one pale face to another along the miserable line of his captives. In a harsh, imperious voice he said something which brought Mansoor, the dragoman, to the front, with bent back and outstretched supplicating palms. To his employers there had always seemed to be something comic in that flapping skirt and short cover-coat above it; but now, under the glare of the mid-day sun, with those faces gathered round them, it appeared rather to add a grotesque horror to the scene. The dragoman salaamed and salaamed like some ungainly automatic doll, and then, as the chief rasped out a curt word or two, he fell suddenly upon his face, rubbing his forehead into the sand, and flapping upon it with his hands.

"What's that, Cochrane?" asked Belmont. "Why is he making an exhibition of himself?"

"As far as I can understand, it is all up with us," the Colonel answered.

"But this is absurd," cried the Frenchman excitedly; "why should these people wish any harm to me? I have never injured them. On the other hand, I have always been their friend. If I could but speak to them, I would make them comprehend. Hola, dragoman, Mansoor!"

The excited gestures of Monsieur Fardet drew the sinister eyes of the Baggara chief upon him. Again he asked a curt question, and Mansoor, kneeling in front of him, answered it.

"Tell him that I am a Frenchman, dragoman. Tell him that I am a friend of the Khalifa. Tell him that my countrymen have never had any quarrel with him, but that his enemies are also ours."

"The chief asks what religion you call your own," said Mansoor. "The Khalifa, he says, has no necessity for any friendship from those who are infidels and unbelievers."

"Tell him that in France we look upon all religions as good."

"The chief says that none but a blaspheming dog and the son of a dog would say that all religions are one as good as the other. He says that if you are indeed the friend of the Khalifa, you will accept the Koran and become a true believer upon the spot. If you will do so he will promise on his side to send you alive to Khartoum."

"And if not?"

"You will fare in the same way as the others."

"Then you may make my compliments to monsieur the chief, and tell him that it is not the custom for Frenchmen to change their religion under compulsion."

The chief said a few words, and then turned to consult with a short, sturdy Arab at his elbow.

"He says, Monsieur Fardet," said the dragoman, "that if you speak again he will make a trough out of you for the dogs to feed from. Say nothing to anger him, sir, for he is now talking what is to be done with us."

"Who is he?" asked the Colonel.

"It is Ali Wad Ibrahim, the same who raided last year, and killed all of the Nubian village."

"I've heard of him," said the Colonel. "He has the name of being one of the boldest and the most fanatical of all the Khalifa's leaders. Thank God that the women are out of his clutches."

The two Arabs had been talking in that stern, restrained fashion which comes so strangely from a southern race. Now they both turned to the dragoman, who was still kneeling upon the sand. They plied him with questions, pointing first to one and then to another of their prisoners. Then they conferred together once more, and finally said something to Mansoor, with a contemptuous wave of the hand to indicate that he might convey it to the others.

"Thank Heaven, gentlemen, I think that we are saved for the present time," said Mansoor, wiping away the sand which had stuck to his perspiring forehead. "Ali Wad Ibrahim says that though an unbeliever should have only the edge of the sword from one of the sons of the Prophet, yet it might be of more profit to the beit-el-mal at Omdurman if it had the gold which your people will pay for you. Until it comes you can work as the slaves of the Khalifa, unless he should decide to put you to death. You are to mount yourselves upon the spare camels and to ride with the party."

The chief had waited for the end of the explanation. "Now he gave a brief order, and a negro stepped forward with a long, dull-coloured sword in his hand. The dragoman squealed like a rabbit who sees a ferret, and threw himself frantically down upon the sand once more.

"What is it, Cochrane?" asked Cecil Brown—for the Colonel had served in the East, and was the only one of the travellers who had a smattering of Arabic.

"As far as I can make out, he says there is no use keeping the dragoman, as no one would trouble to pay a ransom for him, and he is too fat to make a good slave."

"Poor devil!" cried Brown. "Here, Cochrane, tell them to let him go. We can't let him be butchered like this in front of us. Say that we will find the money amongst us. I will be answerable for any reasonable sum."

"I'll stand in as far as my means will allow," cried Belmont.

"We will sign a joint bond or indemnity," said the lawyer. "If I had a paper and pencil I could throw it into shape in an instant, and the chief could rely upon its being perfectly correct and valid."

But the Colonel's Arabic was insufficient, and Mansoor himself was too maddened by fear to understand the offer which was being made for him. The negro looked a question at the chief, and then his long black arm swung upwards and his sword hissed over his shoulder. But the dragoman had screamed out something which arrested the blow, and which brought the chief and the lieutenant to his side with a new interest upon their swarthy faces. The others crowded in also, and formed a dense circle around the grovelling, pleading man.

The Colonel had not understood this sudden change, nor had the others fathomed the reason of it, but some instinct flashed it upon Stephens's horrified perceptions.

"Oh, you villain!" he cried furiously. "Hold your tongue, you miserable creature! Be silent! Better die—a thousand times better die!"

But it was too late, and already they could all see the base design by which the coward hoped to save his own life. He was about to betray the women. They saw the chief, with a brave man's contempt upon his stern face, make a sign of haughty assent, and then Mansoor spoke rapidly and earnestly, pointing up the hill. At a word from the Baggara, a dozen of the raiders rushed up the path and were lost to view upon the top. Then came a shrill cry, a horrible strenuous scream of surprise and terror, and an instant later the party streamed into sight again, dragging the women in their midst.

Sadie, with her young, active limbs, kept up with them, as they sprang down the slope, encouraging her aunt all the while over her shoulder. The older lady, struggling amid the rushing white figures, looked with her thin limbs and open mouth like a chicken being dragged from a coop.

The chief's dark eyes glanced indifferently at Miss Adams, but gazed with a smouldering fire at the younger woman. Then he gave an abrupt order, and the prisoners were hurried in a miserable, hopeless drove to the cluster of kneeling camels. Their pockets had already been ransacked, and the contents thrown into one of the camel-food bags, the neck of which was tied up by Ali Wad Ibrahim's own hands.

"I say, Cochrane," whispered Belmont, looking with smouldering eyes at the wretched Mansoor, "I've got a little hip revolver which they have not discovered. Shall I shoot that cursed dragoman for giving away the women?"

The Colonel shook his head.

"You had better keep it," said he, with a sombre face. "The women may find some other use for it before all is over."

V

The camels, some brown and some white, were kneeling in a long line, their champing jaws moving rhythmically from side to side, and their gracefully poised heads turning to right and left in a mincing, self-conscious fashion. Most of them were beautiful creatures, true Arabian trotters, with the slim limbs and finely turned necks which mark the breed; but among them were a few of the slower, heavier beasts, with ungroomed skins, disfigured by the black scars of old firings. These were loaded with the doora and the waterskins of the raiders, but a few minutes sufficed to redistribute their loads and to make place for the prisoners. None of these had been bound with the exception of Mr. Stuart—for the Arabs, understanding that he was a clergyman, and accustomed to associate religion with violence, had looked upon his fierce outburst as quite natural, and regarded him now as the most dangerous and enterprising of their captives. His hands were therefore tied together with a plaited camel-halter, but the others, including the dragoman and the two wounded blacks, were allowed to mount without any precaution against their escape, save that which was afforded by the slowness of their beasts. Then, with a shouting of men and a roaring of camels, the creatures were jolted on to their legs, and the long, straggling procession set off with its back to the homely river, and its face to the shimmering, violet haze, which hung round the huge sweep of beautiful, terrible desert, striped tiger-fashion with black rock and with golden sand.

None of the white prisoners, with the exception of Colonel Cochrane, had ever been upon a camel before. It seemed an alarming distance to the ground when they looked down, and the curious swaying motion, with the insecurity of the saddle, made them sick and frightened. But their bodily discomfort was forgotten in the turmoil of bitter thoughts within. What a chasm gaped between their old life and their new! And yet how short was the time and space which divided them! Less than an hour ago they had stood upon the summit of that rock, and had laughed and chattered, or grumbled at the heat and flies, becoming peevish at small discomforts. Headingly had been hypercritical over the tints of Nature. They could not forget his own tint as he lay with his cheek upon the black stone. Sadie had chattered about tailor-made dresses and Parisian chiffons. Now she was clinging, half-crazy, to the pommel of a wooden saddle, with suicide rising as a red star of hope in her mind. Humanity, reason, argument—all were gone, and there remained the brutal humiliation of force. And all the time, down there by the second rocky point, their steamer was waiting for them—their saloon, with the white napery and the glittering glasses, the latest novel, and the London papers. The least imaginative of them could see it so clearly: the white awning, Mrs. Shlesinger with her yellow sun-hat, Mrs. Belmont lying back in the canvas chair. There it lay almost in sight of them, that little floating chip broken off from home, and every silent, ungainly step of the camels was carrying them more hopelessly away from it. That very morning how beneficent Providence had appeared, how pleasant was life!—a little commonplace, perhaps, but so soothing and restful. And now!

The red head-gear, patched jibbehs, and yellow boots had already shown to the Colonel that these men were no wandering party of robbers, but a troop from the regular army of the Khalifa. Now, as they struck across the desert, they showed that they possessed the rude discipline which their work demanded. A mile ahead, and far out on either flank, rode their scouts, dipping and rising among the yellow sand-hills. Ali Wad Ibrahim headed the caravan, and his short, sturdy lieutenant brought up the rear. The main party straggled over a couple of hundred yards, and in the middle was the little, dejected clump of prisoners. No attempt was made to keep them apart, and Mr. Stephens soon contrived that his camel should be between those of the two ladies.

"Don't be down-hearted, Miss Adams," said he. "This is a most indefensible outrage, but there can be no question that steps will be taken in the proper quarter to set the matter right. I am convinced that we shall be subjected to nothing worse than a temporary inconvenience. If it had not been for that villain Mansoor, you need not have appeared at all."

It was shocking to see the change in the little Bostonian lady, for she had shrunk to an old woman in an hour. Her swarthy cheeks had fallen in, and her eyes shone wildly from sunken, darkened sockets. Her frightened glances were continually turned upon Sadie. There is surely some wrecker angel which can only gather her best treasures in moments of disaster. For here were all these worldlings going to their doom, and already frivolity and selfishness had passed away from them, and each was thinking and grieving only for the other. Sadie thought of her aunt, her aunt thought of Sadie, the men thought of the women, Belmont thought of his wife—and then he thought of something else also, and he kicked his camel's shoulder with his heel, until he found himself upon the near side of Miss Adams.

"I've got something for you here," he whispered. "We may be separated soon, so it is as well to make our arrangements."

"Separated!" wailed Miss Adams.

"Don't speak loud, for that infernal Mansoor may give us away again. I hope it won't be so, but it might. We must be prepared for the worst. For example, they might determine to get rid of us men and to keep you."

Miss Adams shuddered.

"What am I to do? For God's sake tell me what I am to do, Mr. Belmont! I am an old woman. I have had my day. I could stand it if it was only myself. But Sadie—I am clean crazed when I think of her. There's her mother waiting at home, and I—"She clasped her thin hands together in the agony of her thoughts.

"Put your hand out under your dust-cloak," said Belmont, sidling his camel up against hers. "Don't miss your grip of it. There! Now hide it in your dress, and you'll always have a key to unlock any door."

Miss Adams felt what it was which he had slipped into her hand, and she looked at him for a moment in bewilderment. Then she pursed up her lips and shook her stern, brown face in disapproval. But she pushed the little pistol into its hiding-place, all the same, and she rode with her thoughts in a whirl. Could this indeed be she, Eliza Adams, of Boston, whose narrow, happy life had oscillated between the comfortable house in Commonwealth Avenue and the Tremont Presbyterian Church? Here she was, hunched upon a camel, with her hand upon the butt of a pistol, and her mind weighing the justifications of murder. Oh, life, sly, sleek, treacherous life, how are we ever to trust you? Show us your worst and we can face it, but it is when you are sweetest and smoothest that we have most to fear from you.

"At the worst, Miss Sadie, it will only be a question of ransom," said Stephens, arguing against his own convictions. "Besides, we are still dose to Egypt, far away from the Dervish country. There is sure to be an energetic pursuit. You must try not to lose your courage, and to hope for the best."

"No, I am not scared, Mr. Stephens," said Sadie, turning towards him a blanched face which belied her words. "We're all in God's hands, and surely He won't be cruel to us. It is easy to talk about trusting Him when things are going well, but now is the real test. If He's up there behind that blue heaven—"

"He is," said a voice behind them, and they found that the Birmingham clergyman had joined the party. His tied hands clutched on to his Makloofa saddle, and his fat body swayed dangerously from side to side with every stride of the camel. His wounded leg was oozing with blood and clotted with flies, and the burning desert sun beat down upon his bare head, for he had lost both hat and umbrella in the scuffle. A rising fever flecked his large, white cheeks with a touch of colour, and brought a light into his brown ox-eyes. He had always seemed a somewhat gross and vulgar person to his fellow-travellers. Now, this bitter healing draught of sorrow had transformed him. He was purified, spiritualised, exalted. He had become so calmly strong that he made the others feel stronger as they looked upon him. He spoke of life and of death, of the present, and their hopes of the future; and the black cloud of their misery began to show a golden rift or two. Cecil Brown shrugged his shoulders, for he could not change in an hour the convictions of his life;but the others, even Fardet, the Frenchman, were touched and strengthened. They all took off their hats when he prayed. Then the Colonel made a turban out of his red silk cummerbund, and insisted that Mr. Stuart should wear it. With his homely dress and gorgeous headgear, he looked like a man who has dressed up to amuse the children.

And now the dull, ceaseless, insufferable torment of thirst was added to the aching weariness which came from the motion of the camels. The sun glared down upon them, and then up again from the yellow sand, and the great plain shimmered and glowed until they felt as if they were riding over a cooling sheet of molten metal. Their lips were parched and dried, and their tongues like tags of leather. They lisped curiously in their speech, for it was only the vowel sounds which would come without an effort. Miss Adams's chin had dropped upon her chest, and her great hat concealed her face.

"Auntie will faint if she does not get water," said Sadie. "Oh, Mr. Stephens, is there nothing we could do?"

The Dervishes riding near were all Baggara with the exception of one negro —an uncouth fellow with a face pitted with small-pox. His expression seemed good-natured when compared with that of his Arab comrades, and Stephens ventured to touch his elbow and to point to his water-skin, and then to the exhausted lady. The negro shook his head brusquely, but at the same time he glanced significantly towards the Arabs, as if to say that, if it were not for them, he might act differently. Then he laid his black forefinger upon the breast of his jibbeh.

"Tippy Tilly," said he.

"What's that?" asked Colonel Cochrane.

"Tippy Tilly," repeated the negro, sinking his voice as if he wished only the prisoners to hear him.

The Colonel shook his head.

"My Arabic won't bear much strain. I don't know what he is saying," said he.

"Tippy Tilly. Hicks Pasha," the negro repeated.

"I believe the fellow is friendly to us, but I can't quite make him out," said Cochrane to Belmont. "Do you think that he means that his name is Tippy Tilly, and that he killed Hicks Pasha?"

The negro showed his great white teeth at hearing his own words coming back to him. "Aiwa!" said he. "Tippy Tilly—Bimbashi Mormer—Boum!"

"By Jove, I've got it!" cried Belmont. "He's trying to speak English. Tippy Tilly is as near as he can get to Egyptian Artillery. He has served in the Egyptian Artillery under Bimbashi Mortimer. He was taken prisoner when Hicks Pasha was destroyed, and had to turn Dervish to save his skin. How's that?"

The Colonel said a few words of Arabic and received a reply, but two of the Arabs closed up, and the negro quickened his pace and left them.

"You are quite right," said the Colonel. "The fellow is friendly to us, and would rather fight for the Khedive than for the Khalifa. I don't know that he can do us any good, but I've been in worse holes than this, and come out right side up. After all, we are not out of reach of pursuit, and won't be for another forty-eight hours."

Belmont calculated the matter out in his slow, deliberate fashion.

"It was about twelve that we were on the rock," said he. "They would become alarmed aboard the steamer if we did not appear at two."

"Yes," the Colonel interrupted, "that was to be our lunch hour. I remember saying that when I came back I would have—O Lord, it's best not to think of it!"

"The reis was a sleepy old crock," Belmont continued, "but I have absolute confidence in the promptness and decision of my wife. She would insist upon an immediate alarm being given. Suppose they started back at two-thirty, they should be at Halfa by three, since the journey is down stream. How long did they say that it took to turn out the Camel Corps?"

"Give them an hour."

"And another hour to get them across the river. They would be at the Abousir Rock and pick up the tracks by six o'clock. After that it is a clear race. We are only four hours ahead, and some of these beasts are very spent. We may be saved yet, Cochrane!"

"Some of us may. I don't expect to see the padre alive to-morrow, nor Miss Adams either. They are not made for this sort of thing either of them. Then again we must not forget that these people have a trick of murdering their prisoners when they see that there is a chance of a rescue. See here, Belmont, in case you get back and I don't, there's a matter of a mortgage that I want you to set right for me." They rode on with their shoulders inclined to each other, deep in the details of business.

The friendly negro who had talked of himself as Tippy Tilly had managed to slip a piece of cloth soaked in water into the hand of Mr. Stephens, and Miss Adams had moistened her lips with it. Even the few drops had given her renewed strength, and now that the first crushing shock was over, her wiry, elastic, Yankee nature began to reassert itself.

"These people don't look as if they would harm us, Mr. Stephens," said she. "I guess they have a working religion of their own, such as it is, and that what's wrong to us is wrong to them."

Stephens shook his head in silence. He had seen the death of the donkey- boys, and she had not.

"Maybe we are sent to guide them into a better path," said the old lady. "Maybe we are specially singled out for a good work among them."

If it were not for her niece her energetic and enterprising temperament was capable Of glorying in the chance of evangelising Khartoum, and turning Omdurman into a little well-drained broad-avenued replica of a New England town.

"Do you know what I am thinking of all the time?" said Sadie. "You remember that temple that we saw—when was it? Why, it was this morning. "

They gave an exclamation of surprise, all three of them. Yes, it had been this morning; and it seemed away and away in some dim past experience of their lives, so vast was the change, so new and so overpowering the thoughts which had come between. They rode in silence, full of this strange expansion of time, until at last Stephens reminded Sadie that she had left her remark unfinished.

"Oh yes; it was the wall picture on that temple that I was thinking of. Do you remember the poor string of prisoners who are being dragged along to the feet of the great king—how dejected they looked among the warriors who led them? Who could—who could have thought that within three hours the same fate should be our own? And Mr. Headingly—" She turned her face away and began to cry.

"Don't take on, Sadie," said her aunt; "remember what the minister said just now, that we are all right there in the hollow of God's hand. Where do you think we are going, Mr. Stephens?"

The red edge of his Baedeker still projected from the lawyer's pocket, for it had not been worth their captor's while to take it. He glanced down at it.

"If they will only leave me this, I will look up a few references when we halt. I have a general idea of the country, for I drew a small map of it the other day. The river runs from south to north, so we must be travelling almost due west. I suppose they feared pursuit if they kept too near the Nile bank. There is a caravan route, I remember, which runs parallel to the river, about seventy miles inland. If we continue in this direction for a day we ought to come to it. There is a line of wells through which it passes. It comes out at Assiout, if I remember right, upon the Egyptian side. On the other side, it leads away into the Dervish country—so, perhaps—"

His words were interrupted by a high, eager voice, which broke suddenly into a torrent of jostling words, words without meaning, pouring strenuously out in angry assertions and foolish repetitions. The pink had deepened to scarlet upon Mr. Stuart's cheeks, his eyes were vacant but brilliant, and he gabbled, gabbled, gabbled as he rode. Kindly mother Nature! she will not let her children be mishandled too far. "This is too much," she says; "this wounded leg, these crusted lips, this anxious, weary mind. Come away for a time, until your body becomes more habitable. "And so she coaxes the mind away into the Nirvana of delirium, while the little cell-workers tinker and toil within to get things better for its homecoming. When you see the veil of cruelty which nature wears, try and peer through it, and you will sometimes catch a glimpse of a very homely, kindly face behind.

The Arab guards looked askance at this sudden outbreak of the clergyman, for it verged upon lunacy, and lunacy is to them a fearsome and supernatural thing. One of them rode forward and spoke with the Emir. When he returned he said something to his comrades, one of whom closed in upon each side of the minister's camel, so as to prevent him from falling. The friendly negro sidled his beast up to the Colonel, and whispered to him.

"We are going to halt presently, Belmont," said Cochrane.

"Thank God! They may give us some water. We can't go on like this."

"I told Tippy Tilly that, if he could help us, we would turn him into a Bimbashi when we got him back into Egypt. I think he's willing enough if he only had the power. By Jove, Belmont, do look back at the river."

Their route, which had lain through sand-strewn khors with jagged, black edges—places up which one would hardly think it possible that a camel could climb—opened out now on to a hard, rolling plain, covered thickly with rounded pebbles, dipping and rising to the violet hills upon the horizon. So regular were the long, brown pebble-strewn curves, that they looked like the dark rollers of some monstrous ground-swell. Here and there a little straggling sage-green tuft of camel-grass sprouted up between the stones. Brown plains and violet hills—nothing else in front of them! Behind lay the black jagged rocks through which they had passed with orange slopes of sand, and then far away a thin line of green to mark the course of the river. How cool and beautiful that green looked in the stark, abominable wilderness! On one side they could see the high rock—the accursed rock which had tempted them to their ruin. On the other the river curved, and the sun gleamed upon the water. Oh, that liquid gleam, and the insurgent animal cravings, the brutal primitive longings, which for the instant took the soul out of all of them! They had lost families, countries, liberty, everything, but it was only of water, water, water, that they could think. Mr. Stuart in his delirium began roaring for oranges, and it was insufferable for them to have to listen to him. Only the rough, sturdy Irishman rose superior to that bodily craving. That gleam of river must be somewhere near Halfa, and his wife might be upon the very water at which he looked. He pulled his hat over his eyes, and rode in gloomy silence, biting at his strong, iron-grey moustache.

Slowly the sun sank towards the west, and their shadows began to trail along the path where their hearts would go. It was cooler, and a desert breeze had sprung up, whispering over the rolling, stone-strewed plain. The Emir at their head had called his lieutenant to his side, and the pair had peered about, their eyes shaded by their hands, looking for some landmark.

Then, with a satisfied grunt, the chief's camel had seemed to break short off at its knees, and then at its hocks, going down in three curious, broken-jointed jerks until its stomach was stretched upon the ground. As each succeeding camel reached the spot it lay down also, until they were all stretched in one long line. The riders sprang off, and laid out the chopped tibbin upon cloths in front of them, for no well-bred camel will eat from the ground. In their gentle eyes, their quiet, leisurely way of eating, and their condescending, mincing manner, there was something both feminine and genteel, as though a party of prim old maids had foregathered in the heart of the Libyan Desert.

There was no interference with the prisoners, either male or female, for how could they escape in the centre of that huge plain? The Emir came towards them once, and stood combing out his blue-black beard with his fingers, and looking thoughtfully at them out of his dark, sinister eyes. Miss Adams saw with a shudder that it was always upon Sadie that his gaze was fixed. Then, seeing their distress, he gave an order, and a negro brought a water-skin, from which he gave each of them about half a tumblerful. It was hot and muddy, and tasted of leather, but oh how delightful it was to their parched palates! The Emir said a few abrupt words to the dragoman, and left.

"Ladies and gentlemen," Mansoor began, with something of his old consequential manner; but a glare from the Colonel's eyes struck the words from his lips, and he broke away into a long, whimpering excuse for his conduct.

"How could I do anything otherwise," he wailed, "with the very knife at my throat?"

"You will have the very rope round your throat if we all see Egypt again," growled Cochrane savagely. "In the meantime—"

"That's all right, Colonel," said Belmont. "But for our own sakes we ought to know what the chief has said."

"For my part I'll have nothing to do with the blackguard."

"I think that that is going too far. We are bound to hear what he has to say." Cochrane shrugged his shoulders. Privations had made him irritable, and he had to bite his lip to keep down a bitter answer. He walked slowly away, with his straight-legged military stride.

"What did he say, then?" asked Belmont, looking at the dragoman with an eye which was as stern as the Colonel's.

"He seems to be in a somewhat better manner than before. He said that if he had more water you should have it, but that he is himself short in supply. He said that to-morrow we shall come to the wells of Selimah, and everybody shall have plenty—and the camels too."

"Did he say how long we stopped here?"

"Very little rest, he said, and then forward! Oh, Mr. Belmont—"

"Hold your tongue!" snapped the Irishman, and began once more to count times and distances. If it all worked out as he expected, if his wife had insisted upon the indolent reis giving an instant alarm at Halfa, then the pursuers should be already upon their track. The Camel Corps or the Egyptian Horse would travel by moonlight better and faster than in the day-time. He knew that it was the custom at Halfa to keep at least a squadron of them all ready to start at any instant. He had dined at the mess, and the officers had told him how quickly they could take the field. They had shown him the water-tanks and the food beside each of the beasts, and he had admired the completeness of the arrangements, with little thought as to what it might mean to him in the future. It would be at least an hour before they would all get started again from their present halting-place. That would be a clear hour gained. Perhaps by next morning—

And then, suddenly, his thoughts were terribly interrupted. The Colonel, raving like a madman, appeared upon the crest of the nearest slope, with an Arab hanging on to each of his wrists. His face was purple with rage and excitement, and he tugged and bent and writhed in his furious efforts to get free. "You cursed murderers!" he shrieked, and then, seeing the others in front of him, "Belmont," he cried, "they've killed Cecil Brown."

What had happened was this. In his conflict with his own ill-humour, Cochrane had strolled over this nearest crest, and had found a group of camels in the hollow beyond, with a little knot of angry, loud-voiced men beside them. Brown was the centre of the group, pale, heavy-eyed, with his upturned, spiky moustache and listless manner. They had searched his pockets before, but now they were determined to tear off all his clothes in the hope of finding something which he had secreted. A hideous negro with silver bangles in his ears, grinned and jabbered in the young diplomatist's impassive face. There seemed to the Colonel to be something heroic and almost inhuman in that white calm, and those abstracted eyes. His coat was already open, and the Negro's great black paw flew up to his neck and tore his shirt down to the waist. And at the sound of that r-r-rip, and at the abhorrent touch of those coarse fingers, this man about town, this finished product of the nineteenth century, dropped his life-traditions and became a savage facing a savage. His face flushed, his lips curled back, he chattered his teeth like an ape, and his eyes—those indolent eyes which had always twinkled so placidly—were gorged and frantic. He threw himself upon the negro, and struck him again and again, feebly but viciously, in his broad, black face. He hit like a girl, round arm, with an open palm. The man winced away for an instant, appalled by this sudden blaze of passion. Then with an impatient, snarling cry, he slid a knife from his long loose sleeve and struck upwards under the whirling arm. Brown sat down at the blow and began to cough—to cough as a man coughs who has choked at dinner, furiously, ceaselessly, spasm after spasm. Then the angry red cheeks turned to a mottled pallor, there were liquid sounds in his throat, and, clapping his hand to his mouth, he rolled over on to his side.

The negro, with a brutal grunt of contempt, slid his knife up his sleeve once more, while the Colonel, frantic with impotent anger, was seized by the bystanders, and dragged, raving with fury, back to his forlorn party. His hands were lashed with a camel-halter, and he lay at last, in bitter silence, beside the delirious Nonconformist.

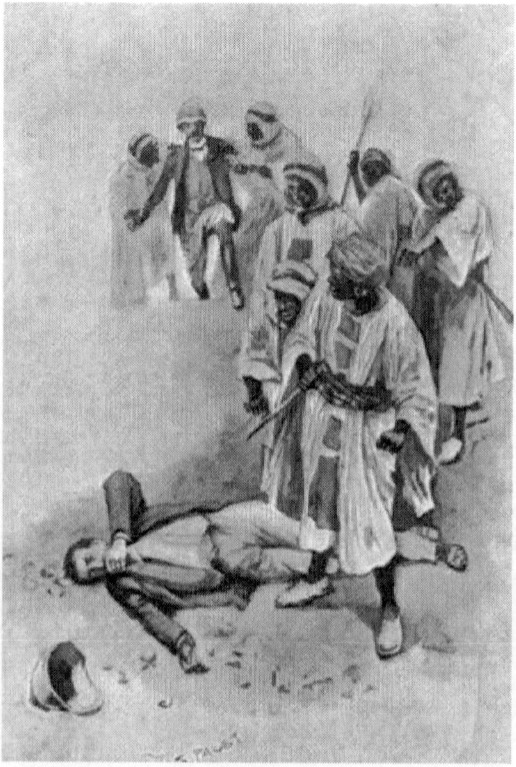

So Headingly was gone, and Cecil Brown was gone, and their haggard eyes were turned from one pale face to another, to know which they should lose next of that frieze of light-hearted riders who had stood out so clearly against the blue morning sky, when viewed from the deck-chairs of the Korosko. Two gone out of ten, and a third out of his mind. The pleasure trip was drawing to its climax.

Fardet, the Frenchman, was sitting alone with his chin resting upon his hands, and his elbows upon his knees, staring miserably out over the desert, when Belmont saw him start suddenly and prick up his head like a dog who hears a strange step. Then, with clenched fingers, he bent his face forward and stared fixedly towards the black eastern hills through which they had passed. Belmont followed his gaze, and, yes-yes—there was something moving there! He saw the twinkle of metal, and the sudden gleam and flutter of some white garment. A Dervish vedette upon the flank turned his camel twice round as a danger signal, and discharged his rifle in the air. The echo of the crack had hardly died away before they were all in their saddles, Arabs and negroes. Another instant, and the camels were on their feet and moving slowly towards the point of alarm. Several armed men surrounded the prisoners, slipping cartridges into their Remingtons as a hint to them to remain still.

"By Heaven, they are men on camels!" cried Cochrane, his troubles all forgotten as he strained his eyes to catch sight of these new-comers. "I do believe that it is our own people." In the confusion he had tugged his hands free from the halter which bound them.

"They've been smarter than I gave them credit for," said Belmont, his eyes shining from under his thick brows. "They are here a long two hours before we could have reasonably expected them. Hurrah, Monsieur Fardet, ca va bien, n'est ce pas?"

"Hurrah, hurrah! merveilleusement bien! Vivent les Anglais! Vivent les Anglais!" yelled the excited Frenchman, as the head of a column of camelry began to wind out from among the rocks.

"See here, Belmont," cried the Colonel. "These fellows will want to shoot us if they see it is all up. I know their ways, and we must be ready for it. Will you be ready to jump on the fellow with the blind eye? and I'll take the big nigger, if I can get my arms round him. Stephens, you must do what you can. You, Fardet, comprenez vous? Il est necessaire to plug these Johnnies before they can hurt us. You, dragoman, tell those two Soudanese soldiers that they must be ready—but, but". . . his words died into a murmur, and he swallowed once or twice. "These are Arabs," said he, and it sounded like another voice.

Of all the bitter day, it was the very bitterest moment. Happy Mr. Stuart lay upon the pebbles with his back against the ribs of his camel, and chuckled consumedly at some joke which those busy little cell-workers had come across in their repairs. His fat face was wreathed and creased with merriment. But the others, how sick, how heart-sick, were they all! The women cried. The men turned away in that silence which is beyond tears. Monsieur Fardet fell upon his face, and shook with dry sobbings.

The Arabs were firing their rifles as a welcome to their friends, and the others as they trotted their camels across the open returned the salutes and waved their rifles and lances in the air. They were a smaller band than the first one—not more than thirty—but dressed in the same red headgear and patched jibbehs. One of them carried a small white banner with a scarlet text scrawled across it. But there was something there which drew the eyes and the thoughts of the tourists away from everything else. The same fear gripped at each of their hearts, and the same impulse kept each of them silent. They stared at a swaying white figure half seen amidst the ranks of the desert warriors.

"What's that they have in the middle of them?" cried Stephens at last. "Look, Miss Adams! Surely it is a woman!"

There was something there upon a camel, but it was difficult to catch a glimpse of it. And then suddenly, as the two bodies met, the riders opened out, and they saw it plainly.

"It's a white woman!"

"The steamer has been taken!"

Belmont gave a cry that sounded high above everything.

"Norah, darling," he shouted, "keep your heart up! I'm here, and it is all well!"

VI

So the Korosko had been taken, and the chances of rescue upon which they had reckoned—all those elaborate calculations of hours and distances—were as unsubstantial as the mirage which shimmered upon the horizon. There would be no alarm at Halfa until it was found that the steamer did not return in the evening. Even now, when the Nile was only a thin green band upon the farthest horizon, the pursuit had probably not begun. In a hundred miles, or even less, they would be in the Dervish country. How small, then, was the chance that the Egyptian forces could overtake them. They all sank into a silent, sulky despair, with the exception of Belmont, who was held back by the guards as he strove to go to his wife's assistance.

The two bodies of camel-men had united, and the Arabs, in their grave, dignified fashion, were exchanging salutations and experiences, while the negroes grinned, chattered, and shouted, with the careless good-humour which even the Koran has not been able to alter. The leader of the new-comers was a greybeard, a worn, ascetic, high-nosed old man, abrupt and fierce in his manner, and soldierly in his bearing. The dragoman groaned when he saw him, and flapped his hands miserably with the air of a man who sees trouble accumulating upon trouble.

"It is the Emir Abderrahman," said he. "I fear now that we shall never come to Khartoum alive."

The name meant nothing to the others, but Colonel Cochrane had heard of him as a monster of cruelty and fanaticism, a red-hot Moslem of the old fighting, preaching dispensation, who never hesitated to carry the fierce doctrines of the Koran to their final conclusions. He and the Emir Wad Ibrahim conferred gravely together, their camels side by side, and their red turbans inclined inwards, so that the black beard mingled with the white one. Then they both turned and stared long and fixedly at the poor, head-hanging huddle of prisoners. The younger man pointed and explained, while his senior listened with a sternly impassive face.

"Who's that nice-looking old gentleman in the white beard?" asked Miss Adams, who had been the first to rally from the bitter disappointment.

"That is their leader now," Cochrane answered.

"You don't say that he takes command over that other one?"

"Yes, lady," said the dragoman; "he is now the head of all."

"Well, that's good for us. He puts me in mind of Elder Mathews who was at the Presbyterian Church in Minister Scott's time. Anyhow, I had rather be in his power than in the hands of that black-haired one with the flint eyes. Sadie, dear, you feel better now its cooler, don't you?"

"Yes, auntie; don't you fret about me. How are you yourself?"

"Well, I'm stronger in faith than I was. I set you a poor example, Sadie, for I was clean crazed at first at the suddenness of it all, and at thinking of what your mother, who trusted you to me, would think about it. My land, there'll be some head-lines in the Boston Herald over this! I guess somebody will have to suffer for it."

"Poor Mr. Stuart!" cried Sadie, as the monotonous droning voice of the delirious man came again to their ears. "Come, auntie, and see if we cannot do something to relieve him."

"I'm uneasy about Mrs. Shlesinger and the child," said Colonel Cochrane. "I can see your wife, Belmont, but I can see no one else."

"They are bringing her over," cried he. "Thank God! We shall hear all about it. They haven't hurt you, Norah, have they?" He ran forward to grasp and kiss the hand which his wife held down to him as he helped her from the camel.

The kind grey eyes and calm sweet face of the Irishwoman brought comfort and hope to the whole party. She was a devout Roman Catholic, and it is a creed which forms an excellent prop in hours of danger. To her, to the Anglican Colonel, to the Nonconformist minister, to the Presbyterian American, even to the two Pagan black riflemen, religion in its various forms was fulfilling the same beneficent office—whispering always that the worst which the world can do is a small thing, and that, however harsh the ways of Providence may seem, it is, on the whole, the wisest and best thing for us that we should go cheerfully whither the Great Hand guides us. They had not a dogma in common, these fellows in misfortune; but they held the intimate, deep-lying spirit, the calm, essential fatalism which is the world-old framework of religion, with fresh crops of dogmas growing like ephemeral lichens upon its granite surface.

"You poor things!" she said. "I can see that you have had a much worse time than I have. No, really, John, dear, I am quite well—not even very thirsty, for our party filled their water-skins at the Nile, and they let me have as much as I wanted. But I don't see Mr. Headingly and Mr. Brown. And poor Mr. Stuart—what a state he has been reduced to!"

"Headingly and Brown are out of their troubles," her husband answered. "You don't know how often I have thanked God to-day, Norah, that you were not with us. And here you are, after all."

"Where should I be but by my husband's side? I had much, much rather be here than safe at Halfa."

"Has any news gone to the town?" asked the Colonel.

"One boat escaped. Mrs. Shlesinger and her child and maid were in it. I was downstairs in my cabin when the Arabs rushed on to the vessel. Those on deck had time to escape, for the boat was alongside. I don't know whether any of them were hit. The Arabs fired at them for some time."

"Did they?" cried Belmont exultantly, his responsive Irish nature catching the sunshine in an instant. "Then, be Jove, we'll do them yet, for the garrison must have heard the firing. What d'ye think, Cochrane? They must be full cry upon our scent this four hours. Any minute we might see the white puggaree of a British officer coming over that rise."

But disappointment had left the Colonel cold and sceptical.

"They need not come at all unless they come strong," said he. "These fellows are picked men with good leaders, and on their own ground they will take a lot of beating." Suddenly he paused and looked at the Arabs. "By George!" said he, "that's a sight worth seeing!"

The great red sun was down with half its disc slipped behind the violet bank upon the horizon. It was the hour of Arab prayer. An older and more learned civilisation would have turned to that magnificent thing upon the skyline and adored that. But these wild children of the desert were nobler in essentials than the polished Persian. To them the ideal was higher than the material, and it was with their backs to the sun and their faces to the central shrine of their religion that they prayed. And how they prayed, these fanatical Moslems! Rapt, absorbed, with yearning eyes and shining faces, rising, stooping, grovelling with their foreheads upon their praying carpets. Who could doubt, as he watched their strenuous, heart-whole devotion, that here was a great living power in the world, reactionary but tremendous, countless millions all thinking as one from Cape Juby to the confines of China? Let a common wave pass over them, let a great soldier or organiser arise among them to use the grand material at his hand, and who shall say that this may not be the besom with which Providence may sweep the rotten, decadent, impossible, half-hearted south of Europe, as it did a thousand years ago, until it makes room for a sounder stock?

And now as they rose to their feet the bugle rang out, and the prisoners understood that, having travelled all day, they were fated to travel all night also. Belmont groaned, for he had reckoned upon the pursuers catching them up before they left this camp. But the others had already got into the way of accepting the inevitable. A flat Arab loaf had been given to each of them—what effort of the chef of the post-boat had ever tasted like that dry brown bread?—and then, luxury of luxuries, they had a second ration of a glass of water, for the fresh-filled bags of the newcomers had provided an ample supply. If the body would but follow the lead of the soul as readily as the soul does that of the body, what a heaven the earth might be! I Now, with their base material wants satisfied for the instant, their spirits began to sing within them, and they mounted their camels with some sense of the romance of their position. Mr. Stuart remained babbling upon the ground, and the Arabs made no effort to lift him into his saddle. His large, white, upturned face glimmered through the gathering darkness.

"Hi, dragoman, tell them that they are forgetting Mr. Stuart," cried the Colonel.

"No use, sir," said Mansoor. "They say that he is too fat, and that they will not take him any farther. He will die, they say, and why should they trouble about him?"

"Not take him!" cried Cochrane. "Why, the man will perish of hunger and thirst. Where's the Emir? Hi!" he shouted, as the black-bearded Arab passed, with a tone like that in which he used to summon a dilatory donkey-boy. The chief did not deign to answer him, but said something to one of the guards, who dashed the butt of his Remington into the Colonel's ribs.

The old soldier fell forward gasping, and was carried on half senseless, clutching at the pommel of his saddle. The women began to cry, and the men, with muttered curses and clenched hands, writhed in that hell of impotent passion, where brutal injustice and ill-usage have to go without check or even remonstrance. Belmont gripped at his hip-pocket for his little revolver, and then remembered that he had already given it to Miss Adams. If his hot hand had clutched it, it would have meant the death of the Emir and the massacre of the party.

And now as they rode onwards they saw one of the most singular of the phenomena of the Egyptian desert in front of them, though the ill-treatment of their companion had left them in no humour for the appreciation of its beauty. When the sun had sunk, the horizon had remained of a slaty-violet hue. But now this began to lighten and to brighten until a curious false dawn developed, and it seemed as if a vacillating sun was coming back along the path which it had just abandoned. A rosy pink hung over the west, with beautifully delicate sea-green tints along the upper edge of it. Slowly these faded into slate again, and the night had come. It was but twenty-four hours since they had sat in their canvas chairs discussing politics by starlight on the saloon deck of the Korosko; only twelve since they had breakfasted there and had started spruce and fresh upon their last pleasure trip. What a world of fresh impressions had come upon them since then! How rudely they had been jostled out of their take-it-for-granted complacency! The same shimmering silver stars, as they had looked upon last night, the same thin crescent of moon—but they, what a chasm lay between that old pampered life and this!

The long line of camels moved as noiselessly as ghosts across the desert. Before and behind were the silent, swaying white figures of the Arabs. Not a sound anywhere, not the very faintest sound, until far away behind them they heard a human voice singing in a strong, droning, unmusical fashion. It had the strangest effect, this far-away voice, in that huge inarticulate wilderness. And then there came a well-known rhythm into that distant chant, and they could almost hear the words—

We nightly pitch our moving tent, A day's march nearer home.

Was Mr. Stuart in his right mind again, or was it some coincidence of his delirium, that he should have chosen this for his song? With moist eyes his friends looked back through the darkness, for well they knew that home was very near to this wanderer. Gradually the voice died away into a hum, and was absorbed once more into the masterful silence of the desert.

"My dear old chap, I hope you're not hurt?" said Belmont, laying his hand upon Cochrane's knee.

The Colonel had straightened himself, though he still gasped a little in his breathing.

"I am all right again, now. Would you kindly show me which was the man who struck me?"

"It was the fellow in front there—with his camel beside Fardet's. "

"The young fellow with the moustache—I can't see him very well in this light, but I think I could pick him out again. Thank you, Belmont!"

"But I thought some of your ribs were gone."

"No, it only knocked the wind out of me."

"You must be made of iron. It was a frightful blow. How could you rally from it so quickly?"

The Colonel cleared his throat and hummed and stammered.

"The fact is, my dear Belmont—I'm sure you would not let it go further—above all not to the ladies; but I am rather older than I used to be, and rather than lose the military carriage which has always been dear to me, I—"

"Stays, be Jove!" cried the astonished Irishman.

"Well, some slight artificial support," said the Colonel stiffly, and switched the conversation off to the chances of the morrow.

It still comes back in their dreams to those who are left, that long night's march in the desert. It was like a dream itself, the silence of it as they were borne forward upon those soft, shuffling sponge feet, and the flitting, flickering figures which oscillated upon every side of them. The whole universe seemed to be hung as a monstrous time-dial in front of them. A star would glimmer like a lantern on the very level of their path. They looked again, and it was a hand's-breadth up, and another was shining beneath it. Hour after hour the broad stream flowed sedately across the deep blue background, worlds and systems drifting majestically overhead, and pouring over the dark horizon. In their vastness and their beauty there was a vague consolation to the prisoners; for their own fate, and their own individuality, seemed trivial and unimportant amid the play of such tremendous forces. Slowly the grand procession swept across the heaven, first climbing, then hanging long with little apparent motion, and then sinking grandly downwards, until away in the east the first cold grey glimmer appeared, and their own haggard faces shocked each other's sight.

The day had tortured them with its heat, and now the night had brought the even more intolerable discomfort of cold. The Arabs swathed themselves in their gowns and wrapped up their heads. The prisoners beat their hands together and shivered miserably. Miss Adams felt it most, for she was very thin, with the impaired circulation of age. Stephens slipped off his Norfolk jacket and threw it over her shoulders. He rode beside Sadie, and whistled and chatted to make here believe that her aunt was really relieving him by carrying his jacket for him, but the attempt was too boisterous not to be obvious; and yet it was so far true that he probably felt the cold less than any of the party, for the old, old fire was burning in his heart, and a curious joy was inextricably mixed with all his misfortunes, so that he would have found it hard to say if this adventure had been the greatest evil or the greatest blessing of his lifetime. Aboard the boat, Sadie's youth, her beauty, her intelligence and humour, all made him realise that she could at the best only be expected to charitably endure him. But now he felt that he was really of some use to her, that every hour she was learning to turn to him as one turns to one's natural protector; and above all, he had begun to find himself—to understand that there really was a strong, reliable man behind all the tricks of custom which had built up an artificial nature, which had imposed even upon himself. A little glow of self-respect began to warm his blood. He had missed his youth when he was young, and now in his middle age it was coming up like some beautiful belated flower.

"I do believe that you are all the time enjoying it, Mr. Stephens," said Sadie with some bitterness.

"I would not go so far as to say that," he answered. "But I am quite certain that I would not leave you here."

It was the nearest approach to tenderness which he had ever put into a speech, and the girl looked at him in surprise.

"I think I've been a very wicked girl all my life," she said after a pause. "Because I have had a good time myself, I never thought of those who were unhappy. This has struck me serious. If ever I get back I shall be a better woman—a more earnest woman—in the future."

"And I a better man. I suppose it is just for that that trouble comes to us. Look how it has brought out the virtues of all our friends. Take poor Mr. Stuart, for example. Should we ever have known what a noble, constant man he was? And see Belmont and his wife, in front of us there, going fearlessly forward, hand in hand, thinking only of each other. And Cochrane, who always seemed on board the boat to be a rather stand-offish, narrow sort of man! Look at his courage, and his unselfish indignation when any one is ill used. Fardet, too, is as brave as a lion. I think misfortune has done us all good."

Sadie sighed.

"Yes, if it would end right here one might say so; but if it goes on and on for a few weeks or months of misery, and then ends in death, I don't know where we reap the benefit of those improvements of character which it brings. Suppose you escape, what will you do?"

The lawyer hesitated, but his professional instincts were still strong.

"I will consider whether an action lies, and against whom. It should be with the organisers of the expedition for taking us to the Abousir Rock — or else with the Egyptian Government for not protecting their frontiers. It will be a nice legal question. And what will you do, Sadie?"

It was the first time that he had ever dropped the formal Miss, but the girl was too much in earnest to notice it.

"I will be more tender to others," she said. "I will try to make some one else happy in memory of the miseries which I have endured."

"You have done nothing all your life but made others happy. You cannot help doing it," said he. The darkness made it more easy for him to break through the reserve which was habitual with him. "You need this rough schooling far less than any of us. How could your character be changed for the better?"

"You show how little you know me. I have been very selfish and thoughtless."

"At least you had no need for all these strong emotions. You were sufficiently alive without them. Now it has been different with me."

"Why did you need emotions, Mr. Stephens?"

"Because anything is better than stagnation. Pain is better than stagnation. I have only just begun to live. Hitherto I have been a machine upon the earth's surface. I was a one-ideaed man, and a one-ideaed man is only one remove from a dead man. That is what I have only just begun to realise. For all these years I have never been stirred, never felt a real throb of human emotion pass through me. I had no time for it. I had observed it in others, and I had vaguely wondered whether there was some want in me which prevented my sharing the experience of my fellow-mortals. But now these last few days have taught me how keenly I can live—that I can have warm hopes, and deadly fears—that I can hate, and that I can— well, that I can have every strong feeling which the soul can experience. I have come to life. I may be on the brink of the grave, but at least I can say now that I have lived."

"And why did you lead this soul-killing life in England?"

"I was ambitious—I wanted to get on. And then there were my mother and my sisters to be thought of. Thank Heaven, here is the morning coming. Your aunt and you will soon cease to feel the cold."

"And you without your coat!"

"Oh, I have a very good circulation. I can manage very well in my shirt-sleeves."

And now the long, cold, weary night was over, and the deep blue-black sky had lightened to a wonderful mauve-violet, with the larger stars still glinting brightly out of it. Behind them the grey line had crept higher and higher, deepening into a delicate rose-pink, with the fan-like rays of the invisible sun shooting and quivering across it. Then, suddenly, they felt its warm touch upon their backs, and there were hard black shadows upon the sand in front of them. The Dervishes loosened their cloaks and proceeded to talk cheerily among themselves. The prisoners also began to thaw, and eagerly ate the doora which was served out for their breakfasts. A short halt had been called, and a cup of water handed to each.

"Can I speak to you, Colonel Cochrane?" asked the dragoman.

"No, you can't," snapped the Colonel.

"But it is very important—all our safety may come from it."

The Colonel frowned and pulled at his moustache.

"Well, what is it?" he asked at last.

"You must trust to me, for it is as much to me as to you to get back to Egypt. My wife and home, and children, are on one part, and a slave for life upon the other. You have no cause to doubt it."

"Well, go on!"

"You know the black man who spoke with you—the one who had been with Hicks?"

"Yes, what of him?"

"He has been speaking with me during the night. I have had a long talk with him. He said that he could not very well understand you, nor you him, and so he came to me."

"What did he say?"

"He said that there were eight Egyptian soldiers among the Arabs— six black and two fellaheen. He said that he wished to have your promise that they should all have very good reward if they helped you to escape."

"Of course they shall."

"They asked for one hundred Egyptian pounds each."

"They shall have it."

"I told him that I would ask you, but that I was sure that you would agree to it."

"What do they propose to do?"

"They could promise nothing, but what they thought best was that they should ride their camels not very far from you, so that if any chance should come they would be ready to take advantage."

"Well, you can go to him and promise two hundred pounds each if they will help us. You do not think we could buy over some Arabs?"

Mansoor shook his head. "Too much danger to try," said he. "Suppose you try and fail, then that will be the end to all of us. I will go tell what you have said." He strolled off to where the old negro gunner was grooming his camel and waiting for his reply.

The Emirs had intended to halt for a half-hour at the most, but the baggage-camels which bore the prisoners were so worn out with the long, rapid march, that it was clearly impossible that they should move for some time. They had laid their long necks upon the ground, which is the last symptom of fatigue. The two chiefs shook their heads when they inspected them, and the terrible old man looked with his hard-lined, rock features at the captives. Then he said something to Mansoor, whose face turned a shade more sallow as he listened.

"The Emir Abderrahman says that if you do not become Moslem, it is not worth while delaying the whole caravan in order to carry you upon the baggage-camels. If it were not for you, he says that we could travel twice as fast. He wishes to know therefore, once for ever, if you will accept the Koran. "Then in the same tone, as if he were still translating, he continued: "You had far better consent, for if you do not he will most certainly put you all to death."

The unhappy prisoners looked at each other in despair. The two Emirs stood gravely watching them.

"For my part," said Cochrane, "I had as soon die now as be a slave in Khartoum."

"What do you say, Norah?" asked Belmont.

"If we die together, John, I don't think I shall be afraid."

"It is absurd that I should die for that in which I have never had belief," said Fardet. "And yet it is not possible for the honour of a Frenchman that he should be converted in this fashion." He drew himself up, with his wounded wrist stuck into the front of his jacket, "Je suis Chretien. J'y reste," he cried, a gallant falsehood in each sentence.

"What do you say, Mr. Stephens?" asked Mansoor in a beseeching voice. "If one of you would change, it might place them in a good humour. I implore you that you do what they ask."

"No, I can't," said the lawyer quietly.

"Well then, you, Miss Sadie? You, Miss Adams? It is only just to say it once, and you will be saved."

"Oh, auntie, do you think we might?" whimpered the frightened girl. "Would it be so very wrong if we said it?"

The old lady threw her arms round her. "No, no, my own dear little Sadie," she whispered. "You'll be strong! You would just hate yourself for ever after. Keep your grip of me, dear, and pray if you find your strength is leaving you. Don't forget that your old aunt Eliza has you all the time by the hand."

For an instant they were heroic, this line of dishevelled, bedraggled pleasure-seekers. They were all looking Death in the face, and the closer they looked the less they feared him. They were conscious rather of a feeling of curiosity, together with the nervous tingling with which one approaches a dentist's chair. The dragoman made a motion of his hands and shoulders, as one who has tried and failed. The Emir Abderrahman said something to a negro, who hurried away.

"What does he want a scissors for?" asked the Colonel.

"He is going to hurt the women," said Mansoor, with the same gesture of impotence.

A cold chill fell upon them all. They stared about them in helpless horror. Death in the abstract was one thing, but these insufferable details were another. Each had been braced to endure any evil in his own person, but their hearts were still soft for each other. The women said nothing, but the men were all buzzing together.

"There's the pistol, Miss Adams," said Belmont. "Give it here! We won't be tortured! We won't stand it!"

"Offer them money, Mansoor! Offer them anything!" cried Stephens. "Look here, I'll turn Mohammedan if they'll promise to leave the women alone. After all, it isn't binding—it's under compulsion. But I can't see the women hurt."

"No, wait a bit, Stephens!" said the Colonel. "We mustn't lose our heads. I think I see a way out. See here, dragoman! You tell that grey-bearded old devil that we know nothing about his cursed tinpot religion. Put it smooth when you translate it. Tell him that he cannot expect us to adopt it until we know what particular brand of rot it is that he wants us to believe. Tell him that if he will instruct us, we are perfectly willing to listen to his teaching, and you can add that any creed which turns out such beauties as him, and that other bounder with the black beard, must claim the attention of every one."

With bows and suppliant sweepings of his hands the dragoman explained that the Christians were already full of doubt, and that it needed but a little more light of knowledge to guide them on to the path of Allah. The two Emirs stroked their beards and gazed suspiciously at them.

Then Abderrahman spoke in his crisp, stern fashion to the dragoman, and the two strode away together. An instant later the bugle rang out as a signal to mount.

"What he says is this," Mansoor explained, as he rode in the middle of the prisoners. "We shall reach the wells by mid-day, and there will be a rest. His own Moolah, a very good and learned man, will come to give you an hour of teaching. At the end of that time you will choose one way or the other. When you have chosen, it will be decided whether you are to go to Khartoum or to be put to death. That is his last word."

"They won't take ransom?"

"Wad Ibrahim would, but the Emir Abderrahman is a terrible man. I advise you to give in to him."

"What have you done yourself? You are a Christian, too."

Mansoor blushed as deeply as his complexion would allow.

"I was yesterday morning. Perhaps I will be to-morrow morning. I serve the Lord as long as what He ask seem reasonable; but this is very otherwise. "

He rode onwards amongst the guards with a freedom which showed that his change of faith had put him upon a very different footing to the other prisoners.

So they were to have a reprieve of a few hours, though they rode in that dark shadow of death which was closing in upon them. What is there in life that we should cling to it so? It is not the pleasures, for those whose hours are one long pain shrink away screaming when they see merciful Death holding his soothing arms out for them. It is not the associations, for we will change all of them before we walk of our own free-wills down that broad road which every son and daughter of man must tread. Is it the fear of losing the I, that dear, intimate I, which we think we know so well, although it is eternally doing things which surprise us? Is it that which makes the deliberate suicide cling madly to the bridge-pier as the river sweeps him by? Or is it that Nature is so afraid that all her weary workmen may suddenly throw down their tools and strike, that she has invented this fashion of keeping them constant to their present work? But there it is, and all these tired, harassed, humiliated folk rejoiced in the few more hours of suffering which were left to them.

VII

There was nothing to show them as they journeyed onwards that they were not on the very spot that they had passed at sunset upon the evening before. The region of fantastic black hills and orange sand which bordered the river had long been left behind, and everywhere now was the same brown, rolling, gravelly plain, the ground-swell with the shining rounded pebbles upon its surface, and the occasional little sprouts of sage-green camel-grass. Behind and before it extended, to where far away in front of them it sloped upwards towards a line of violet hills. The sun was not high enough yet to cause the tropical shimmer, and the wide landscape, brown with its violet edging, stood out with a hard clearness in that dry, pure air. The long caravan straggled along at the slow swing of the baggage-camels. Far out on the flanks rode the vedettes, halting at every rise, and peering backwards with their hands shading their eyes. In the distance their spears and rifles seemed to stick out of them, straight and thin, like needles in knitting.

"How far do you suppose we are from the Nile?" asked Cochrane. He rode with his chin on his shoulder and his eyes straining wistfully to the eastern skyline.

"A good fifty miles," Belmont answered.

"Not so much as that," said the Colonel. "We could not have been moving more than fifteen or sixteen hours, and a camel does not do more than two and a half miles an hour unless it is trotting. That would only give about forty miles, but still it is, I fear, rather far for a rescue. I don't know that we are much the better for this postponement. What have we to hope for? We may just as well take our gruel."

"Never say die!" cried the cheery Irishman. "There's plenty of time between this and mid-day. Hamilton and Hedley of the Camel Corps are good boys, and they'll be after us like a streak. They'll have no baggage-camels to hold them back, you can lay your life on that! Little did I think, when I dined with them at mess that last night, and they were telling me all their precautions against a raid, that I should depend upon them for our lives."

"Well, we'll play the game out, but I'm not very hopeful," said Cochrane. "Of course, we must keep the best face we can before the women. I see that Tippy Tilly is as good as his word, for those five niggers and the two brown Johnnies must be the men he speaks of. They all ride together and keep well up, but I can't see how they are going to help us."

"I've got my pistol back," whispered Belmont, and his square chin and strong mouth set like granite. "If they try any games on the women, I mean to shoot them all three with my own hand, and then we'll die with our minds easy. "

"Good man!" said Cochrane, and they rode on in silence. None of them spoke much. A curious, dreamy, irresponsible feeling crept over them. It was as if they had all taken some narcotic drug—the merciful anodyne which Nature uses when a great crisis has fretted the nerves too far. They thought of their friends and of their past lives in the comprehensive way in which one views that which is completed. A subtle sweetness mingled with the sadness of their fate. They were filled with the quiet serenity of despair.

"It's devilish pretty," said the Colonel, looking about him. "I always had an idea that I should like to die in a real, good, yellow London fog. You couldn't change for the worse."

"I should have liked to have died in my sleep," said Sadie. "How beautiful to wake up and find yourself in the other world! There was a piece that Hetty Smith used to say at the College: 'Say not good-night, but in some brighter world wish me good-morning.'"

The Puritan aunt shook her head at the idea. "It's a terrible thing to go unprepared into the presence of your Maker," said she.

"It's the loneliness of death that is terrible," said Mrs. Belmont. "If we and those whom we loved all passed over simultaneously, we should think no more of it than of changing our house."

"If the worst comes to the worst, we won't be lonely," said her husband. "We'll all go together, and we shall find Brown and Headingly and Stuart waiting on the other side."

The Frenchman shrugged his shoulders. He had no belief in survival after death, but he envied the two Catholics the quiet way in which they took things for granted. He chuckled to think of what his friends in the Cafe Cubat would say if they learned that he had laid down his life for the Christian faith. Sometimes it amused and sometimes it maddened him, and he rode onwards with alternate gusts of laughter and of fury, nursing his wounded wrist all the time like a mother with a sick baby.

Across the brown of the hard, pebbly desert there had been visible for some time a single long, thin, yellow streak, extending north and south as far as they could see. It was a band of sand not more than a few hundred yards across, and rising at the highest to eight or ten feet. But the prisoners were astonished to observe that the Arabs pointed at this with an air of the utmost concern, and they halted when they came to the edge of it like men upon the brink of an unfordable river. It was very light, dusty sand, and every wandering breath of wind sent it dancing into the air like a whirl of midges. The Emir Abderrahman tried to force his camel into it, but the creature, after a step or two, stood still and shivered with terror.

The two chiefs talked for a little, and then the whole caravan trailed off with their heads for the north, and the streak of sand upon their left.

"What is it?" asked Belmont, who found the dragoman riding at his elbow. "Why are we going out of our course?"

"Drift sand," Mansoor answered. "Every sometimes the wind bring it all in one long place like that. To-morrow, if a wind comes, perhaps there will not be one grain left, but all will be carried up into the air again. An Arab will sometimes have to go fifty or a hundred miles to go round a drift. Suppose he tries to cross, his camel breaks its legs, and he himself is sucked in and swallowed."

"How long will this be?"

"No one can say."

"Well, Cochrane, it's all in our favour. The longer the chase the better chance for the fresh camels!" and for the hundredth time he looked back at the long, hard skyline behind them. There was the great, empty, dun-coloured desert, but where the glint of steel or the twinkle of white helmet for which he yearned?

And soon they cleared the obstacle in their front. It spindled away into nothing, as a streak of dust would which has been blown across an empty room. It was curious to see that when it was so narrow that one could almost jump it, the Arabs would still go for many hundreds of yards rather than risk the crossing. Then, with good, hard country before them once more, the tired beasts were whipped up, and they ambled on with a double-jointed jogtrot, which set the prisoners nodding and bowing in grotesque and ludicrous misery. It was fun at first, and they smiled at each other, but soon the fun had become tragedy as the terrible camel-ache seized them by spine and waist, with its deep, dull throb, which rises gradually to a splitting agony.

"I can't stand it, Sadie," cried Miss Adams suddenly. "I've done my best. I'm going to fall."

"No, no, auntie, you'll break your limbs if you do. Hold up, just a little, and maybe they'll stop."

"Lean back, and hold your saddle behind," said the Colonel. "There, you'll find that will ease the strain. "He took the puggaree from his hat, and tying the ends together, he slung it over her front pommel. "Put your foot in the loop," said he. "It will steady you like a stirrup."

The relief was instant, so Stephens did the same for Sadie. But presently one of the weary doora camels came down with a crash, its limbs starred out as if it had split asunder, and the caravan had to come down to its old sober gait.

"Is this another belt of drift sand?" asked the Colonel presently.

"No, it's white," said Belmont. "Here, Mansoor, what is that in front of us?"

But the dragoman shook his head.

"I don't know what it is, sir. I never saw the same thing before."

Right across the desert, from north to south, there was drawn a white line, as straight and clear as if it had been slashed with chalk across a brown table. It was very thin, but it extended without a break from horizon to horizon. Tippy Tilly said something to the dragoman.

"It's the great caravan route," said Mansoor.

"What makes it white, then?"

"The bones."

It seemed incredible, and yet it was true, for as they drew nearer they saw that it was indeed a beaten track across the desert, hollowed out by long usage, and so covered with bones that they gave the impression of a continuous white ribbon. Long, snouty heads were scattered everywhere, and the lines of ribs were so continuous that it looked in places like the framework of a monstrous serpent. The endless road gleamed in the sun as if it were paved with ivory. For thousands of years this had been the highway over the desert, and during all that time no animal of all those countless caravans had died there without being preserved by the dry, antiseptic air. No wonder, then, that it was hardly possible to walk down it now without treading upon their skeletons.

"This must be the route I spoke of," said Stephens. "I remember marking it upon the map I made for you, Miss Adams. Baedeker says that it has been disused on account of the cessation of all trade which followed the rise of the Dervishes, but that it used to be the main road by which the skins and gums of Darfur found their way down to Lower Egypt."

They looked at it with a listless curiosity, for there was enough to engross them at present in their own fates. The caravan struck to the south along the old desert track, and this Golgotha of a road seemed to be a fitting avenue for that which awaited them at the end of it. Weary camels and weary riders dragged on together towards their miserable goal.

And now, as the critical moment approached which was to decide their fate, Colonel Cochrane, weighed down by his fears lest something terrible should befall the women, put his pride aside to the extent of asking the advice of the renegade dragoman. The fellow was a villain and a coward, but at least he was an Oriental, and he understood the Arab point of view. His change of religion had brought him into closer contact with the Dervishes, and he had overheard their intimate talk. Cochrane's stiff, aristocratic nature fought hard before he could bring himself to ask advice from such a man, and when he at last did so, it was in the gruffest and most unconciliatory voice.

"You know the rascals, and you have the same way of looking at things," said he. "Our object is to keep things going for another twenty-four hours. After that it does not much matter what befalls us, for we shall be out of the reach of rescue. But how can we stave them off for another day?"

"You know my advice," the dragoman answered; "I have already answered it to you. If you will all become as I have, you will certainly be carried to Khartoum in safety. If you do not, you will never leave our next camping-place alive."

The Colonel's well-curved nose took a higher tilt, and an angry flush reddened his thin cheeks. He rode in silence for a little, for his Indian service had left him with a curried-prawn temper, which had had an extra touch of cayenne added to it by his recent experiences. It was some minutes before he could trust himself to reply.

"We'll set that aside," said he at last. "Some things are possible and some are not. This is not."

"You need only pretend."

"That's enough," said the Colonel abruptly.

Mansoor shrugged his shoulders.

"What is the use of asking me, if you become angry when I answer? If you do not wish to do what I say, then try your own attempt. At least you cannot say that I have not done all I could to save you."

"I'm not angry," the Colonel answered after a pause, in a more conciliatory voice, "but this is climbing down rather farther than we care to go. Now, what I thought is this. You might, if you chose, give this priest, or Moolah, who is coming to us, a hint that we really are softening a bit upon the point. I don't think, considering the hole that we are in, that there can be very much objection to that. Then, when he comes, we might play up and take an interest and ask for more instruction, and in that way hold the matter over for a day or two. Don't you think that would be the best game?"

"You will do as you like," said Mansoor. "I have told you once for ever what I think. If you wish that I speak to the Moolah, I will do so. It is the fat, little man with the grey beard, upon the brown camel in front there. I may tell you that he has a name among them for converting the infidel, and he has a great pride in it, so that he would certainly prefer that you were not injured if he thought that he might bring you into Islam."

"Tell him that our minds are open, then," said the Colonel. "I don't suppose the padre would have gone so far, but now that he is dead I think we may stretch a point. You go to him, Mansoor, and if you work it well we will agree to forget what is past. By the way, has Tippy Tilly said anything?"

"No, sir. He has kept his men together, but he does not understand yet how he can help you."

"Neither do I. Well, you go to the Moolah, then, and I'll tell the others what we have agreed."

The prisoners all acquiesced in the Colonel's plan, with the exception of the old New England lady, who absolutely refused even to show any interest in the Mohammedan creed. "I guess I am too old to bow the knee to Baal," she said. The most that she would concede was that she would not openly interfere with anything which her companions might say or do.

"And who is to argue with the priest?" asked Fardet, as they all rode together, talking the matter over. "It is very important that it should be done in a natural way, for if he thought that we were only trying to gain time, he would refuse to have any more to say to us."

"I think Cochrane should do it, as the proposal is his," said Belmont.

"Pardon me!" cried the Frenchman. "I will not say a word against our friend the Colonel, but it is not possible that a man should be fitted for everything. It will all come to nothing if he attempts it. The priest will see through the Colonel."

"Will he?" said the Colonel with dignity.

"Yes, my friend, he will, for, like most of your countrymen, you are very wanting in sympathy for the ideas of other people, and it is the great fault which I find with you as a nation."

"Oh, drop the politics!" cried Belmont impatiently.

"I do not talk politics. What I say is very practical. How can Colonel Cochrane pretend to this priest that he is really interested in his religion when, in effect, there is no religion in the world to him outside some little church in which he has been born and bred? I will say this for the Colonel, that I do not believe he is at all a hypocrite, and I am sure that he could not act well enough to deceive such a man as this priest."

The Colonel sat with a very stiff back and the blank face of a man who is not quite sure whether he is being complimented or insulted.

"You can do the talking yourself if you like," said he at last. "I should he very glad to be relieved of it."

"I think that I am best fitted for it, since I am equally interested in all creeds. When I ask for information, it is because in verity I desire it, and not because I am playing a part."

"I certainly think that it would be much better if Monsieur Fardet would undertake it," said Mrs. Belmont with decision, and so the matter was arranged.

The sun was now high, and it shone with dazzling brightness upon the bleached bones which lay upon the road. Again the torture of thirst fell upon the little group of survivors, and again, as they rode with withered tongues and crusted lips, a vision of the saloon of the Korosko danced like a mirage before their eyes, and they saw the white napery, the wine-cards by the places, the long necks of the bottles, the siphons upon the sideboard. Sadie, who had borne up so well, became suddenly hysterical, and her shrieks of senseless laughter jarred horribly upon their nerves. Her aunt on one side of her, and Mr. Stephens on the other, did all they could to soothe her, and at last the weary, overstrung girl relapsed into something between a sleep and a faint, hanging limp over her pommel, and only kept from falling by the friends who clustered round her. The baggage-camels were as weary as their riders, and again and again they had to jerk at their nose-ropes to prevent them from lying down. From horizon to horizon stretched that one huge arch of speckless blue, and up its monstrous concavity crept the inexorable sun, like some splendid but barbarous deity, who claimed a tribute of human suffering as his immemorial right.

Their course still lay along the old trade route, but their progress was very slow, and more than once the two Emirs rode back together, and shook their heads as they looked at the weary baggage-camels on which the prisoners were perched. The greatest laggard of all was one which was ridden by a wounded Soudanese soldier. It was limping badly with a strained tendon, and it was only by constant prodding that it could be kept with the others. The Emir Wad Ibrahim raised his Remington, as the creature hobbled past, and sent a bullet through its brain. The wounded man flew forwards out of the high saddle, and fell heavily upon the hard track. His companions in misfortune, looking back, saw him stagger to his feet with a dazed face. At the same instant a Baggara slipped down from his camel with a sword in his hand.

"Don't look! don't look!" cried Belmont to the ladies, and they all rode on with their faces to the south. They heard no sound, but the Baggara passed them a few minutes afterwards. He was cleaning his sword upon the hairy neck of his camel, and he glanced at them with a quick, malicious gleam of his teeth as he trotted by. But those who are at the lowest pitch of human misery are at least secured against the future. That vicious, threatening smile which might once have thrilled them left them now unmoved—or stirred them at most to vague resentment. There were many things to interest them in this old trade route, had they been in a condition to take notice of them. Here and there along its course were the crumbling remains of ancient buildings, so old that no date could be assigned to them, but designed in some far-off civilisation to give the travellers shade from the sun or protection from the ever-lawless children of the desert. The mud bricks with which these refuges were constructed showed that the material had been carried over from the distant Nile. Once, upon the top of a little knoll, they saw the shattered plinth of a pillar of red Assouan granite, with the wide-winged symbol of the Egyptian god across it, and the cartouche of the second Rameses beneath. After three thousand years one cannot get away from the ineffaceable footprints of the warrior-king. It is surely the most wonderful survival of history that one should still be able to gaze upon him, high-nosed and masterful, as he lies with his powerful arms crossed upon his chest, majestic even in decay, in the Gizeh Museum. To the captives, the cartouche was a message of hope, as a sign that they were not outside the sphere of Egypt. "They've left their card here once, and they may again," said Belmont, and they all tried to smile.

And now they came upon one of the most satisfying sights on which the human eye can ever rest. Here and there, in the depressions at either side of the road, there had been a thin scurf of green, which meant that water was not very far from the surface. And then, quite suddenly, the track dipped down into a bowl-shaped hollow, with a most dainty group of palm-trees, and a lovely green sward at the bottom of it. The sun gleaming upon that brilliant patch of clear, restful colour, with the dark glow of the bare desert around it, made it shine like the purest emerald in a setting of burnished copper. And then it was not its beauty only, but its promise for the future: water, shade, all that weary travellers could ask for. Even Sadie was revived by the cheery sight, and the spent camels snorted and stepped out more briskly, stretching their long necks and sniffing the air as they went. After the unhomely harshness of the desert, it seemed to all of them that they had never seen anything more beautiful than this. They looked below at the green sward with the dark, star-like shadows of the palm-crowns; then they looked up at those deep green leaves against the rich blue of the sky, and they forgot their impending death in the beauty of that Nature to whose bosom they were about to return.

The wells in the centre of the grove consisted of seven large and two small saucer-like cavities filled with peat-coloured water, enough to form a plentiful supply for any caravan. Camels and men drank it greedily, though it was tainted by the all-pervading natron. The camels were picketed, the Arabs threw their sleeping-mats down in the shade, and the prisoners, after receiving a ration of dates and of doora, were told that they might do what they would during the heat of the day, and that the Moolah would come to them before sunset. The ladies were given the thicker shade of an acacia tree, and the men lay down under the palms. The great green leaves swished slowly above them; they heard the low hum of the Arab talk, and the dull champing of the camels, and then in an instant, by that most mysterious and least understood of miracles, one was in a green Irish valley, and another saw the long straight line of Commonwealth Avenue, and a third was dining at a little round table opposite to the bust of Nelson in the Army and Navy Club, and for him the swishing of the palm branches had been transformed into the long-drawn hum of Pall Mall. So the spirits went their several ways, wandering back along the strange, un-traced tracks of the memory, while the weary, grimy bodies lay senseless under the palm-trees in the Oasis of the Libyan Desert.

VIII

Colonel Cochrane was awakened from his slumber by some one pulling at his shoulder. As his eyes opened they fell upon the black, anxious face of Tippy Tilly, the old Egyptian gunner. His crooked finger was laid upon his thick, liver-coloured lips, and his dark eyes glanced from left to right with ceaseless vigilance.

"Lie quiet! Do not move!" he whispered, in Arabic. "I will lie here beside you, and they cannot tell me from the others. You can understand what I am saying?"

"Yes, if you will talk slowly."

"Very good. I have no great trust in this black man, Mansoor. I had rather talk direct with the Miralai."

"What have you to say?"

"I have waited long, until they should all be asleep, and now in another hour we shall be called to evening prayer. First of all, here is a pistol, that you may not say that you are without arms."

It was a clumsy, old-fashioned thing, but the Colonel saw the glint of a percussion cap upon the nipple, and knew that it was loaded. He slipped it into the inner pocket of his Norfolk jacket.

"Thank you," said he; "speak slowly, so that I may understand you."

"There are eight of us who wish to go to Egypt. There are also four men in your party. One of us, Mehemet Ali, has fastened twelve camels together, which are the fastest of all save only those which are ridden by the Emirs. There are guards upon watch, but they are scattered in all directions. The twelve camels are close beside us here—those twelve behind the acacia tree. If we can only get mounted and started, I do not think that many can overtake us, and we shall have our rifles for them. The guards are not strong enough to stop so many of us. The water-skins are all filled, and we may see the Nile again by to-morrow night."

The Colonel could not follow it all, but he understood enough to set a little spring of hope bubbling in his heart. The last terrible day had left its mark in his livid face and his hair, which was turning rapidly to grey. He might have been the father of the spruce well-preserved soldier who had paced with straight back and military stride up and down the saloon deck of the Korosko.

"That is excellent," said he. "But what are we to do about the three ladies?" The black soldier shrugged his shoulders. "Mefeesh!" said he. "One of them is old, and in any case there are plenty more women if we get back to Egypt. These will not come to any hurt, but they will be placed in the harem of the Khalifa."

"What you say is nonsense," said the Colonel sternly. "We shall take our women with us, or we shall not go at all."

"I think it is rather you who talk the thing without sense," the black man answered angrily. "How can you ask my companions and me to do that which must end in failure? For years we have waited for such a chance as this, and now that it has come, you wish us to throw it away owing to this foolishness about the women."

"What have we promised you if we come back to Egypt?" asked Cochrane.

"Two hundred Egyptian pounds and promotion in the army—all upon the word of an Englishman."

"Very good. Then you shall have three hundred each if you can make some new plan by which you can take the women with you."

Tippy Tilly scratched his woolly head in his perplexity.

"We might, indeed, upon some excuse, bring three more of the faster camels round to this place. Indeed, there are three very good camels among those which are near the cooking fire. But how are we to get the women upon them? —and if we had them upon them, we know very well that they would fall off when they began to gallop. I fear that you men will fall off, for it is no easy matter to remain upon a galloping camel; but as to the women, it is impossible. No, we shall leave the women, and if you will not leave the women, then we shall leave all of you and start by ourselves."

"Very good! Go!" said the Colonel abruptly, and settled down as if to sleep once more. He knew that with Orientals it is the silent man who is most likely to have his way.

The negro turned and crept away for some little distance, where he was met by one of his fellaheen comrades, Mehemet Ali, who had charge of the camels. The two argued for some little time—for those three hundred golden pieces were not to be lightly resigned. Then the negro crept back to Colonel Cochrane.

"Mehemet Ali has agreed," said he. "He has gone to put the nose-rope upon three more of the camels. But it is foolishness, and we are all going to our death. Now come with me, and we shall awaken the women and tell them."

The Colonel shook his companions and whispered to them what was in the wind. Belmont and Fardet were ready for any risk. Stephens, to whom the prospect of a passive death presented little terror, was seized with a convulsion of fear when he thought of any active exertion to avoid it, and shivered in all his long, thin limbs. Then he pulled out his Baedeker and began to write his will upon the flyleaf, but his hand twitched so that he was hardly legible. By some strange gymnastic of the legal mind a death, even by violence, if accepted quietly, had a place in the order of things, while a death which overtook one galloping frantically over a desert was wholly irregular and discomposing. It was not dissolution which he feared, but the humiliation and agony of a fruitless struggle against it.

Colonel Cochrane and Tippy Tilly had crept together under the shadow of the great acacia tree to the spot where the women were lying. Sadie and her aunt lay with their arms round each other, the girl's head pillowed upon the old woman's bosom. Mrs. Belmont was awake, and entered into the scheme in an instant.

"But you must leave me," said Miss Adams earnestly. "What does it matter at my age, anyhow?"

"No, no, Aunt Eliza; I won't move without you! Don't you think it!" cried the girl. "You've got to come straight away or else we both stay right here where we are."

"Come, come, ma'am, there is no time for arguing, or nonsense," said the Colonel roughly. "Our lives all depend upon your making an effort, and we cannot possibly leave you behind."

"But I will fall off."

"I'll tie you on with my puggaree. I wish I had the cummerbund which I lent poor Stuart. Now, Tippy, I think we might make a break for it!"

But the black soldier had been staring with a disconsolate face out over the desert, and he turned upon his heel with an oath.

"There!" said he sullenly. "You see what comes of all your foolish talking! You have ruined our chances as well as your own!"

Half-a-dozen mounted camel-men had appeared suddenly over the lip of the bowl-shaped hollow, standing out hard and clear against the evening sky where the copper basin met its great blue lid. They were travelling fast, and waved their rifles as they came. An instant later the bugle sounded an alarm, and the camp was up with a buzz like an overturned bee-hive. The Colonel ran back to his companions, and the black soldier to his camel. Stephens looked relieved, and Belmont sulky, while Monsieur Fardet raved, with his one uninjured hand in the air.

"Sacred name of a dog!" he cried. "Is there no end to it, then? Are we never to come out of the hands of these accursed Dervishes?"

"Oh, they really are Dervishes, are they?" said the Colonel in an acid voice. "You seem to be altering your opinions. I thought they were an invention of the British Government."

The poor fellows' tempers were getting frayed and thin. The Colonel's sneer was like a match to a magazine, and in an instant the Frenchman was dancing in front of him with a broken torrent of angry words. His hand was clutching at Cochrane's throat before Belmont and Stephens could pull him off.

"If it were not for your grey hairs—" he said.

"Damn your impudence!" cried the Colonel.

"If we have to die, let us die like gentlemen, and not like so many corner-boys," said Belmont with dignity.

"I only said I was glad to see that Monsieur Fardet has learned something from his adventures," the Colonel sneered.

"Shut up, Cochrane! What do you want to aggravate him for?" cried the Irishman.

"Upon my word, Belmont, you forget yourself! I do not permit people to address me in this fashion."

"You should look after your own manners, then."

"Gentlemen, gentlemen, here are the ladies!" cried Stephens, and the angry, over-strained men relapsed into a gloomy silence, pacing up and down, and jerking viciously at their moustaches. It is a very catching thing, ill- temper, for even Stephens began to be angry at their anger, and to scowl at them as they passed him. Here they were at a crisis in their fate, with the shadow of death above them, and yet their minds were all absorbed in some personal grievance so slight that they could hardly put it into words. Misfortune brings the human spirit to a rare height, but the pendulum still swings.

But soon their attention was drawn away to more important matters. A council of war was being held beside the wells, and the two Emirs, stern and composed, were listening to a voluble report from the leader of the patrol. The prisoners noticed that, though the fierce, old man stood like a graven image, the younger Emir passed his hand over his beard once or twice with a nervous gesture, the thin, brown fingers twitching among the long, black hair.

"I believe the Gippies are after us," said Belmont. "Not very far off either, to judge by the fuss they are making."

"It looks like it. Something has scared them."

"Now he's giving orders. What can it be? Here, Mansoor, what is the matter?"

The dragoman came running up with the light of hope shining upon his brown face.

"I think they have seen something to frighten them. I believe that the soldiers are behind us. They have given the order to fill the water-skins, and be ready for a start when the darkness comes. But I am ordered to gather you together, for the Moolah is coming to convert you all. I have already told him that you are all very much inclined to think the same with him."

How far Mansoor may have gone with his assurances may never be known, but the Mussulman preacher came walking towards them at this moment with a paternal and contented smile upon his face, as one who has a pleasant and easy task before him. He was a one-eyed man, with a fringe of grizzled beard and a face which was fat, but which looked as if it had once been fatter, for it was marked with many folds and creases. He had a green turban upon his head, which marked him as a Mecca pilgrim. In one hand he carried a small brown carpet, and in the other a parchment copy of the Koran. Laying his carpet upon the ground, he motioned Mansoor to his side, and then gave a circular sweep of his arm to signify that the prisoners should gather round him, and a downward wave which meant that they should be seated. So they grouped themselves round him, sitting on the short green sward under the palm-tree, these seven forlorn representatives of an alien creed, and in the midst of them sat the fat little preacher, his one eye dancing from face to face as he expounded the principles of his newer, cruder, and more earnest faith. They listened attentively and nodded their heads as Mansoor translated the exhortation, and with each sign of their acquiescence the Moolah became more amiable in his manner and more affectionate in his speech.

"For why should you die, my sweet lambs, when all that is asked of you is that you should set aside that which will carry you to everlasting Gehenna, and accept the law of Allah as written by his prophet, which will assuredly bring you unimaginable joys, as is promised in the Book of the Camel? For what says the chosen one?"—and he broke away into one of those dogmatic texts which pass in every creed as an argument. "Besides, is it not clear that God is with us, since from the beginning, when we had but sticks against the rifles of the Turks, victory has always been with us? Have we not taken El Obeid, and taken Khartoum, and destroyed Hicks and slain Gordon, and prevailed against every one who has come against us? How, then, can it be said that the blessing of Allah does not rest upon us?"

The Colonel had been looking about him during the long exhortation of the Moolah, and he had observed that the Dervishes were cleaning their guns, counting their cartridges, and making all the preparations of men who expected that they might soon be called upon to fight. The two Emirs were conferring together with grave faces, and the leader of the patrol pointed, as he spoke to them, in the direction of Egypt. It was evident that there was at least a chance of a rescue if they could only keep things going for a few more hours. The camels were not recovered yet from their long march, and the pursuers, if they were indeed close behind, were almost certain to overtake them.

"For God's sake, Fardet, try and keep him in play," said he. "I believe we have a chance if we can only keep the ball rolling for another hour or so. "

But a Frenchman's wounded dignity is not so easily appeased. Monsieur Fardet sat moodily with his back against the palm-tree, and his black brows drawn down. He said nothing, but he still pulled at his thick, strong moustache.

"Come on, Fardet! We depend upon you," said Belmont.

"Let Colonel Cochrane do it," the Frenchman answered snappishly. "He takes too much upon himself this Colonel Cochrane."

"There! There!" said Belmont soothingly, as if he were speaking to a fractious child. "I am quite sure that the Colonel will express his regret at what has happened, and will acknowledge that he was in the wrong—"

"I'll do nothing of the sort," snapped the Colonel.

"Besides, that is merely a personal quarrel," Belmont continued hastily. "It is for the good of the whole party that we wish you to speak with the Moolah, because we all feel that you are the best man for the job."

But the Frenchman only shrugged his shoulders and relapsed into a deeper gloom.

The Moolah looked from one to the other, and the kindly expression began to fade away from his large, baggy face. His mouth drew down at the corners, and became hard and severe.

"Have these infidels been playing with us, then?" said he to the dragoman. "Why is it that they talk among themselves and have nothing to say to me?"

"He's getting impatient about it," said Cochrane. "Perhaps I had better do what I can, Belmont, since this damned fellow has left us in the lurch."

But the ready wit of a woman saved the situation.

"I am sure, Monsieur Fardet," said Mrs. Belmont, "that you, who are a Frenchman, and therefore a man of gallantry and honour, would not permit your own wounded feelings to interfere with the fulfilment of your promise and your duty towards three helpless ladies."

Fardet was on his feet in an instant, with his hand over his heart.

"You understand my nature, madame," he cried. "I am incapable of abandoning a lady. I will do all that I can in this matter. Now, Mansoor, you may tell the holy man that I am ready to discuss through you the high matters of his faith with him."

And he did it with an ingenuity which amazed his companions. He took the tone of a man who is strongly attracted, and yet has one single remaining shred of doubt to hold him back. Yet as that one shred was torn away by the Moolah, there was always some other stubborn little point which prevented his absolute acceptance of the faith of Islam. And his questions were all so mixed up with personal compliments to the priest and self-congratulations that they should have come under the teachings of so wise a man and so profound a theologian, that the hanging pouches under the Moolah's eyes quivered with his satisfaction, and he was led happily and hopefully onwards from explanation to explanation, while the blue overhead turned into violet, and the green leaves into black, until the great serene stars shone out once more between the crowns of the palm-trees.

"As to the learning of which you speak, my lamb," said the Moolah, in answer to some argument of Fardet's, "I have myself studied at the University of El Azhar at Cairo, and I know that to which you allude. But the learning of the faithful is not as the learning of the unbeliever, and it is not fitting that we pry too deeply into the ways of Allah. Some stars have tails, oh my sweet lamb, and some have not; but what does it profit us to know which are which? For God made them all, and they are very safe in His hands. Therefore, my friend, be not puffed up by the foolish learning of the West, and understand that there is only one wisdom, which consists in following the will of Allah as His chosen prophet has laid it down for us in this book. And now, my lambs, I see that you are ready to come into Islam, and it is time, for that bugle tells that we are about to march, and it was the order of the excellent Emir Abderrahman that your choice should be taken, one way or the other, before ever we left the wells."

"Yet, my father, there are other points upon which I would gladly have instruction," said the Frenchman, "for, indeed, it is a pleasure to hear your clear words after the cloudy accounts which we have had from other teachers. "

But the Moolah had risen, and a gleam of suspicion twinkled in his single eye.

"This further instruction may well come afterwards," said he, "since we shall travel together as far as Khartoum, and it will be a joy to me to see you grow in wisdom and in virtue as we go. "He walked over to the fire, and stooping down, with the pompous slowness of a stout man, he returned with two half-charred sticks, which he laid cross-wise upon the ground. The Dervishes came clustering over to see the new converts admitted into the fold. They stood round in the dim light, tall and fantastic, with the high necks and supercilious heads of the camels swaying above them.

"Now," said the Moolah, and his voice had lost its conciliatory and persuasive tone, "there is no more time for you. Here upon the ground I have made out of two sticks the foolish and superstitious symbol of your former creed. You will trample upon it, as a sign that you renounce it, and you will kiss the Koran, as a sign that you accept it, and what more you need in the way of instruction shall be given to you as you go."

They stood up, the four men and the three women, to meet the crisis of their fate. None of them, except perhaps Miss Adams and Mrs. Belmont, had any deep religious convictions. All of them were children of this world, and some of them disagreed with everything which that symbol upon the earth represented. But there was the European pride, the pride of the white race which swelled within them, and held them to the faith of their countrymen. It was a sinful, human, un-Christian motive, and yet it was about to make them public martyrs to the Christian creed. In the hush and tension of their nerves low sounds grew suddenly loud upon their ears. Those swishing palm-leaves above them were like a swift-flowing river, and far away they could hear the dull, soft thudding of a galloping camel.

"There's something coming," whispered Cochrane. "Try and stave them off for five minutes longer, Fardet."

The Frenchman stepped out with a courteous wave of his uninjured arm, and the air of a man who is prepared to accommodate himself to anything.

"You will tell this holy man that I am quite ready to accept his teaching, and so I am sure are all my friends," said he to the dragoman. "But there is one thing which I should wish him to do in order to set at rest any possible doubts which may remain in our hearts. Every true religion can be told by the miracles which those who profess it can bring about. Even I who am but a humble Christian, can, by virtue of my religion, do some of these. But you, since your religion is superior, can no doubt do far more, and so I beg you to give us a sign that we may be able to say that we know that the religion of Islam is the more powerful."

Behind all his dignity and reserve, the Arab has a good fund of curiosity. The hush among the listening Arabs showed how the words of the Frenchman as translated by Mansoor appealed to them.

"Such things are in the hands of Allah," said the priest. "It is not for us to disturb His laws. But if you have yourself such powers as you claim, let us be witnesses to them."

The Frenchman stepped forward, and raising his hand he took a large, shining date out of the Moolah's beard. This he swallowed and immediately produced once more from his left elbow. He had often given his little conjuring entertainment on board the boat, and his fellow-passengers had had some good-natured laughter at his expense, for he was not quite skilful enough to deceive the critical European intelligence. But now it looked as if this piece of obvious palming might be the point upon which all their fates would hang. A deep hum of surprise rose from the ring of Arabs, and deepened as the Frenchman drew another date from the nostril of a camel and tossed it into the air, from which, apparently, it never descended. That gaping sleeve was obvious enough to his companions, but the dim light was all in favour of the performer. So delighted and interested was the audience that they paid little heed to a mounted camel-man who trotted swiftly between the palm trunks. All might have been well had not Fardet, carried away by his own success, tried to repeat his trick once more, with the result that the date fell out of his palm, and the deception stood revealed. In vain he tried to pass on at once to another of his little stock. The Moolah said something, and an Arab struck Fardet across the shoulders with the thick shaft of his spear.

"We have had enough child's play," said the angry priest. "Are we men or babes, that you should try to impose upon us in this manner? Here is the cross and the Koran—which shall it be?"

Fardet looked helplessly round at his companions.

"I can do no more; you asked for five minutes. You have had them," said he to Colonel Cochrane.

"And perhaps it is enough," the soldier answered. "Here are the Emirs. "

The camel-man, whose approach they had heard from afar, had made for the two Arab chiefs, and had delivered a brief report to them, stabbing with his forefinger in the direction from which he had come. There was a rapid exchange of words between the Emirs, and then they strode forward together to the group around the prisoners. Bigots and barbarians, they were none the less two most majestic men, as they advanced through the twilight of the palm grove. The fierce old greybeard raised his hand and spoke swiftly in short, abrupt sentences, and his savage followers yelped to him like hounds to a huntsman. The fire that smouldered in his arrogant eyes shone back at him from a hundred others. Here were to be read the strength and danger of the Mahdi movement; here in these convulsed faces, in that fringe of waving arms, in these frantic, red-hot souls, who asked nothing better than a bloody death, if their own hands might be bloody when they met it.

"Have the prisoners embraced the true faith?" asked the Emir Abderrahman, looking at them with his cruel eyes.

The Moolah had his reputation to preserve, and it was not for him to confess to a failure.

"They were about to embrace it, when—

"Let it rest for a little time, O Moolah." He gave an order, and the Arabs all sprang for their camels. The Emir Wad Ibrahim filed off at once with nearly half the party. The others were mounted and ready, with their rifles unslung.

"What's happened?" asked Belmont.

"Things are looking up," cried the Colonel. "By George, I think we are going to come through all right. The Gippy Camel Corps are hot on our trail. "

"How do you know?"

"What else could have scared them?"

"O Colonel, do you really think we shall be saved?" sobbed Sadie. The dull routine of misery through which they had passed had deadened all their nerves until they seemed incapable of any acute sensation, but now this sudden return of hope brought agony with it like the recovery of a frost-bitten limb. Even the strong, self-contained Belmont was filled with doubts and apprehensions. He had been hopeful when there was no sign of relief, and now the approach of it set him trembling.

"Surely they wouldn't come very weak," he cried. "Be Jove, if the Commandant let them come weak, he should be court-martialled."

"Sure we're in God's hands, anyway," said his wife, in her soothing, Irish voice. "Kneel down with me, John, dear, if it's the last time, and pray that, earth or heaven, we may not be divided."

"Don't do that! Don't!" cried the Colonel anxiously, for he saw that the eye of the Moolah was upon them. But it was too late, for the two Roman Catholics had dropped upon their knees and crossed themselves. A spasm of fury passed over the face of the Mussulman priest at this public testimony to the failure of his missionary efforts. He turned and said something to the Emir.

"Stand up!" cried Mansoor. "For your life's sake, stand up! He is asking for leave to put you to death."

"Let him do what he likes!" said the obstinate Irishman; "we will rise when our prayers are finished, and not before."

The Emir stood listening to the Moolah, with his baleful gaze upon the two kneeling figures. Then he gave one or two rapid orders, and four camels were brought forward. The baggage-camels which they had hitherto ridden were standing unsaddled where they had been tethered.

"Don't be a fool, Belmont!" cried the Colonel; "everything depends upon our humouring them. Do get up, Mrs. Belmont! You are only putting their backs up!"

The Frenchman shrugged his shoulders as he looked at them. "Mon Dieu!" he cried, "were there ever such impracticable people? Voila!" he added, with a shriek, as the two American ladies fell upon their knees beside Mrs. Belmont. "It is like the camels—one down, all down! Was ever anything so absurd?"

But Mr. Stephens had knelt down beside Sadie and buried his haggard face in his long, thin hands. Only the Colonel and Monsieur Fardet remained standing. Cochrane looked at the Frenchman with an interrogative eye.

"After all," said he, "it is stupid to pray all your life, and not to pray now when we have nothing to hope for except through the goodness of Providence." He dropped upon his knees with a rigid, military back, but his grizzled, unshaven chin upon his chest. The Frenchman looked at his kneeling companions, and then his eyes travelled onwards to the angry faces of the Emir and Moolah.

"Sapristi!" he growled. "Do they suppose that a Frenchman is afraid of them?" and so, with an ostentatious sign of the cross, he took his place upon his knees beside the others. Foul, bedraggled, and wretched, the seven figures knelt and waited humbly for their fate under the black shadow of the palm-tree.

The Emir turned to the Moolah with a mocking smile, and pointed at the results of his ministrations. Then he gave an order, and in an instant the four men were seized. A couple of deft turns with a camel-halter secured each of their wrists. Fardet screamed out, for the rope had bitten into his open wound. The others took it with the dignity of despair.

"You have ruined everything. I believe you have ruined me also!" cried Mansoor, wringing his hands. "The women are to get upon these three camels."

"Never!" cried Belmont. "We won't be separated!" He plunged madly, but he was weak from privation, and two strong men held him by each elbow.

"Don't fret, John!" cried his wife, as they hurried her towards the camel. "No harm shall come to me. Don't struggle, or they'll hurt you, dear. "

The four men writhed as they saw the women dragged away from them. All their agonies had been nothing to this. Sadie and her aunt appeared to be half senseless from fear. Only Mrs. Belmont kept a brave face. When they were seated the camels rose, and were led under the tree behind where the four men were standing.

"I've a pistol in me pocket," said Belmont, looking up at his wife. "I would give me soul to be able to pass it to you."

"Keep it, John, and it may be useful yet. I have no fears. Ever since we prayed I have felt as if our guardian angels had their wings round us. "She was like a guardian angel herself as she turned to the shrinking Sadie, and coaxed some little hope back into her despairing heart.

The short, thick Arab, who had been in command of Wad Ibrahim's rearguard, had Joined the Emir and the Moolah; the three consulted together, with occasional oblique glances towards the prisoners. Then the Emir spoke to Mansoor.

"The chief wishes to know which of you four is the richest man?" said the dragoman. His fingers were twitching with nervousness and plucking incessantly at the front of his covercoat.

"Why does he wish to know?" asked the Colonel.

"I do not know."

"But it is evident," cried Monsieur Fardet. "He wishes to know which is the best worth keeping for his ransom."

"I think we should see this thing through together," said the Colonel. "It's really for you to decide, Stephens, for I have no doubt that you are the richest of us."

"I don't know that I am," the lawyer answered; "but in any case, I have no wish to be placed upon a different footing to the others."

The Emir spoke again in his harsh rasping voice.

"He says," Mansoor translated, "that the baggage-camels are spent, and that there is only one beast left which can keep up. It is ready now for one of you, and you have to decide among yourselves which is to have it. If one is richer than the others, he will have the preference."

"Tell him that we are all equally rich."

"In that case he says that you are to choose at once which is to have the camel."

"And the others?"

The dragoman shrugged his shoulders.

"Well," said the Colonel, "if only one of us is to escape, I think you fellows will agree with me that it ought to be Belmont, since he is the married man."

"Yes, yes, let it be Monsieur Belmont," cried Fardet.

"I think so also," said Stephens.

But the Irishman would not hear of it.

"No, no, share and share alike," he cried. "All sink or all swim, and the devil take the flincher."

They wrangled among themselves until they became quite heated in this struggle of unselfishness. Some one had said that the Colonel should go because he was the oldest, and the Colonel was a very angry man.

"One would think I was an octogenarian," he cried. "These remarks are quite uncalled for."

"Well, then," said Belmont, "let us all refuse to go."

"But this is not very wise," cried the Frenchman. "See, my friends! Here are the ladies being carried off alone. Surely it would be far better that one of us should be with them to advise them."

They looked at one another in perplexity. What Fardet said was obviously true, but how could one of them desert his comrades? The Emir himself suggested the solution.

"The chief says," said Mansoor, "that if you cannot settle who is to go, you had better leave it to Allah and draw lots."

"I don't think we can do better," said the Colonel, and his three companions nodded their assent.

It was the Moolah who approached them with four splinters of palm-bark protruding from between his fingers.

"He says that he who draws the longest has the camel," said Mansoor.

"We must agree to abide absolutely by this," said Cochrane, and again his companions nodded.

The Dervishes had formed a semicircle in front of them, with a fringe of the oscillating heads of the camels. Before them was a cooking fire, which threw its red light over the group. The Emir was standing with his back to it, and his fierce face towards the prisoners. Behind the four men was a line of guards, and behind them again the three women, who looked down from their camels upon this tragedy. With a malicious smile, the fat, one-eyed Moolah advanced with his fist closed, and the four little brown spicules protruding from between his fingers.

It was to Belmont that he held them first. The Irishman gave an involuntary groan, and his wife gasped behind him, for the splinter came away in his hand. Then it was the Frenchman's turn, and his was half an inch longer than Belmont's. Then came Colonel Cochrane, whose piece was longer than the two others put together. Stephens' was no bigger than Belmont's. The Colonel was the winner of this terrible lottery.

"You're welcome to my place, Belmont," said he. "I've neither wife nor child, and hardly a friend in the world. Go with your wife, and I'll stay."

"No, indeed! An agreement is an agreement. It's all fair play, and the prize to the luckiest."

"The Emir says that you are to mount at once," said Mansoor, and an Arab dragged the Colonel by his wrist-rope to the waiting camel.

"He will stay with the rearguard," said the Emir to his lieutenant. "You can keep the women with you also."

"And this dragoman dog?"

"Put him with the others."

"And they?"

"Put them all to death."

IX

As none of the three could understand Arabic, the order of the Emir would have been unintelligible to them had it not been for the conduct of Mansoor. The unfortunate dragoman, after all his treachery and all his subservience and apostasy, found his worst fears realised when the Dervish leader gave his curt command. With a shriek of fear the poor wretch threw himself forward upon his face, and clutched at the edge of the Arab's jibbeh, clawing with his brown fingers at the edge of the cotton skirt. The Emir tugged to free himself, and then, finding that he was still held by that convulsive grip, he turned and kicked at Mansoor with the vicious impatience with which one drives off a pestering cur. The dragoman's high red tarboosh flew up into the air, and he lay groaning upon his face where the stunning blow of the Arab's horny foot had left him.

All was bustle and movement in the camp, for the old Emir had mounted his camel, and some of his party were already beginning to follow their companions. The squat lieutenant, the Moolah, and about a dozen Dervishes surrounded the prisoners. They had not mounted their camels, for they were told off to be the ministers of death. The three men understood as they looked upon their faces that the sand was running very low in the glass of their lives. Their hands were still bound, but their guards had ceased to hold them. They turned round, all three, and said good-bye to the women upon the camels.

"All up now, Norah," said Belmont. "It's hard luck when there was a chance of a rescue, but we've done our best."

For the first time his wife had broken down. She was sobbing convulsively, with her face between her hands.

"Don't cry, little woman! We've had a good time together. Give my love to all friends at Bray! Remember me to Amy McCarthy and to the Blessingtons. You'll find there is enough and to spare, but I would take Roger's advice about the investments. Mind that!"

"O John, I won't live without you!" Sorrow for her sorrow broke the strong man down, and he buried his face in the hairy side of her camel. The two of them sobbed helplessly together.

Stephens meanwhile had pushed his way to Sadie's beast. She saw his worn earnest face looking up at her through the dim light.

"Don't be afraid for your aunt and for yourself," said he. "I am sure that you will escape. Colonel Cochrane will look after you. The Egyptians cannot be far behind. I do hope you will have a good drink before you leave the wells. I wish I could give your aunt my jacket, for it will be cold to-night. I'm afraid I can't get it off. She should keep some of the bread, and eat it in the early morning."

He spoke quite quietly, like a man who is arranging the details of a picnic. A sudden glow of admiration for this quietly consistent man warmed her impulsive heart.

"How unselfish you are!" she cried. "I never saw any one like you. Talk about saints! There you stand in the very presence of death, and you think only of us."

"I want to say a last word to you, Sadie, if you don't mind. I should die so much happier. I have often wanted to speak to you, but I thought that perhaps you would laugh, for you never took anything very seriously, did you? That was quite natural of course with your high spirits, but still it was very serious to me. But now I am really a dead man, so it does not matter very much what I say."

"Oh don't, Mr. Stephens!" cried the girl.

"I won't, if it is very painful to you. As I said, it would make me die happier, but I don't want to be selfish about it. If I thought it would darken your life afterwards, or be a sad recollection to you, I would not say another word."

"What did you wish to say?"

"It was only to tell you how I loved you. I always loved you. From the first I was a different man when I was with you. But of course it was absurd, I knew that well enough. I never said anything, but I tried not to make myself ridiculous. But I just want you to know about it now that it can't matter one way or the other. You'll understand that I really do love you when I tell you that, if it were not that I knew you were frightened and unhappy, these last two days in which we have been always together would have been infinitely the happiest of my life."

The girl sat pale and silent, looking down with wondering eyes at his upturned face. She did not know what to do or say in the solemn presence of this love which burned so brightly under the shadow of death. To her child's heart it seemed incomprehensible—and yet she understood that it was sweet and beautiful also.

"I won't say any more," said he; "I can see that it only bothers you. But I wanted you to know, and now you do know, so it is all right. Thank you for listening so patiently and gently. Good-bye, little Sadie! I can't put my hand up. Will you put yours down?"

She did so and Stephens kissed it. Then he turned and took his place once more between Belmont and Fardet. In his whole life of struggle and success he had never felt such a glow of quiet contentment as suffused him at that instant when the grip of death was closing upon him. There is no arguing about love. It is the innermost fact of life—the one which obscures and changes all the others, the only one which is absolutely satisfying and complete. Pain is pleasure, and want is comfort, and death is sweetness when once that golden mist is round it. So it was that Stephens could have sung with joy as he faced his murderers. He really had not time to think about them. The important, all-engrossing, delightful thing was that she could not look upon him as a casual acquaintance any more. Through all her life she would think of him—she would know.

Colonel Cochrane's camel was at one side, and the old soldier, whose wrists had been freed, had been looking down upon the scene, and wondering in his tenacious way whether all hope must really be abandoned. It was evident that the Arabs who were grouped round the victims were to remain behind with them, while the others who were mounted would guard the three women and himself. He could not understand why the throats of his companions had not been already cut, unless it were that with an Eastern refinement of cruelty this rearguard would wait until the Egyptians were close to them, so that the warm bodies of their victims might be an insult to the pursuers. No doubt that was the right explanation. The Colonel had heard of such a trick before.

But in that case there would not be more than twelve Arabs with the prisoners. Were there any of the friendly ones among them? If Tippy Tilly and six of his men were there, and if Belmont could get his arms free and his hand upon his revolver, they might come through yet. The Colonel craned his neck and groaned in his disappointment. He could see the faces of the guards in the firelight. They were all Baggara Arabs, men who were beyond either pity or bribery. Tippy Tilly and the others must have gone on with the advance. For the first time the stiff old soldier abandoned hope.

"Good-bye, you fellows! God bless you!" he cried, as a negro pulled at his camel's nose-ring and made him follow the others. The women came after him, in a misery too deep for words. Their departure was a relief to the three men who were left.

"I am glad they are gone," said Stephens, from his heart.

"Yes, yes, it is better," cried Fardet. "How long are we to wait?"

"Not very long now," said Belmont grimly, as the Arabs closed in around them.

The Colonel and the three women gave one backward glance when they came to the edge of the oasis. Between the straight stems of the palms they saw the gleam of the fire, and above the group of Arabs they caught a last glimpse of the three white hats. An instant later, the camels began to trot, and when they looked back once more the palm grove was only a black clump with the vague twinkle of a light somewhere in the heart of it. As with yearning eyes they gazed at that throbbing red point in the darkness, they passed over the edge of the depression, and in an instant the huge, silent, moonlit desert was round them without a sign of the oasis which they had left. On every side the velvet, blue-black sky, with its blazing stars, sloped downwards to the vast, dun-coloured plain. The two were blurred into one at their point of junction.

The women had sat in the silence of despair, and the Colonel had been silent also—for what could he say?—but suddenly all four started in their saddles, and Sadie gave a sharp cry of dismay. In the hush of the night there had come from behind them the petulant crack of a rifle, then another, then several together, with a brisk rat-tat-tat, and then after an interval, one more.

"It may be the rescuers! It may be the Egyptians!" cried Mrs. Belmont, with a sudden flicker of hope. "Colonel Cochrane, don't you think it may be the Egyptians?"

"Yes, yes," Sadie whimpered. "It must be the Egyptians."

The Colonel had listened expectantly, but all was silent again. Then he took his hat off with a solemn gesture.

"There is no use deceiving ourselves, Mrs. Belmont," said he; "we may as well face the truth. Our friends are gone from us, but they have met their end like brave men."

"But why should they fire their guns? They had. . . they had spears." She shuddered as she said it.

"That is true," said the Colonel. "I would not for the world take away any real grounds of hope which you may have; but on the other hand, there is no use in preparing bitter disappointments for ourselves. If we had been listening to an attack, we should have heard some reply. Besides, an Egyptian attack would have been an attack in force. No doubt it is, as you say, a little strange that they should have wasted their cartridges—by Jove, look at that!"

He was pointing over the eastern desert. Two figures were moving across its expanse, swiftly and stealthily, furtive dark shadows against the lighter ground. They saw them dimly, dipping and rising over the rolling desert, now lost, now reappearing in the uncertain light. They were flying away from the Arabs. And then, suddenly they halted upon the summit of a sand-hill, and the prisoners could see them outlined plainly against the sky. They were camel-men, but they sat their camels astride as a horseman sits his horse.

"Gippy Camel Corps!" cried the Colonel.

"Two men," said Miss Adams, in a voice of despair.

"Only a vedette, ma'am! Throwing feelers out all over the desert. This is one of them. Main body ten miles off, as likely as not. There they go giving the alarm! Good old Camel Corps!"

The self-contained, methodical soldier had suddenly turned almost inarticulate with his excitement. There was a red flash upon the top of the sand-hill, and then another, followed by the crack of the rifles. Then with a whisk the two figures were gone, as swiftly and silently as two trout in a stream.

The Arabs had halted for an instant, as if uncertain whether they should delay their journey to pursue them or not. There was nothing left to pursue now, for amid the undulations of the sand-drift the vedettes might have gone in any direction. The Emir galloped back along the line, with exhortations and orders. Then the camels began to trot, and the hopes of the prisoners were dulled by the agonies of the terrible jolt. Mile after mile, mile after mile, they sped onwards over that vast expanse, the women clinging as best they might to the pommels, the Colonel almost as spent as they, but still keenly on the look-out for any sign of the pursuers.

"I think. . . I think," cried Mrs. Belmont, "that something is moving in front of us."

The Colonel raised himself upon his saddle, and screened his eyes from the moonshine.

"By Jove, you're right there, ma'am. There are men over yonder."

They could all see them now, a straggling line of riders far ahead of them in the desert.

"They are going in the same direction as we," cried Mrs. Belmont, whose eyes were very much better than the Colonel's.

Cochrane muttered an oath into his moustache.

"Look at the tracks there," said he; "of course, it's our own vanguard who left the palm grove before us. The chief keeps us at this infernal pace in order to close up with them."

As they drew closer they could see plainly that it was indeed the other body of Arabs, and presently the Emir Wad Ibrahim came trotting back to take counsel with the Emir Abderrahman. They pointed in the direction in which the vedettes had appeared, and shook their heads like men who have many and grave misgivings. Then the raiders joined into one long, straggling line, and the whole body moved steadily on towards the Southern Cross, which was twinkling just over the skyline in front of them. Hour after hour the dreadful trot continued, while the fainting ladies clung on convulsively, and Cochrane, worn out but indomitable, encouraged them to hold out, and peered backwards over the desert for the first glad signs of their pursuers. The blood throbbed in his temples, and he cried that he heard the roll of drums coming out of the darkness. In his feverish delirium he saw clouds of pursuers at their very heels, and during the long night he was for ever crying glad tidings which ended in disappointment and heartache. The rise of the sun showed the desert stretching away around them with nothing moving upon its monstrous face except themselves. With dull eyes and heavy hearts they stared round at that huge and empty expanse. Their hopes thinned away like the light morning mist upon the horizon.

It was shocking to the ladies to look at their companion, and to think of the spruce, hale old soldier who had been their fellow-passenger from Cairo. As in the case of Miss Adams, old age seemed to have pounced upon him in one spring. His hair, which had grizzled hour by hour during his privations, was now of a silvery white. White stubble, too, had obscured the firm, clean line of his chin and throat. The veins of his face were injected, and his features were shot with heavy wrinkles. He rode with his back arched and his chin sunk upon his breast, for the old, time-rotted body was worn out, but in his bright, alert eyes there was always a trace of the gallant tenant who lived in the shattered house. Delirious, spent, and dying, he preserved his chivalrous, protecting air as he turned to the ladies, shot little scraps of advice and encouragement at them, and peered back continually for the help which never came.

An hour after sunrise the raiders called a halt, and food and water were served out to all. Then at a more moderate pace they pursued their southern journey, their long, straggling line trailing out over a quarter of a mile of desert. From their more careless bearing and the way in which they chatted as they rode, it was clear that they thought that they had shaken off their pursuers. Their direction now was east as well as south, and it was evidently their intention after this long detour to strike the Nile again at some point far above the Egyptian outposts. Already the character of the scenery was changing, and they were losing the long levels of the pebbly desert, and coming once more upon those fantastic, sunburned, black rocks, and that rich orange sand through which they had already passed. On every side of them rose the scaly, conical hills with their loose, slag-like debris, and jagged-edged khors, with sinuous streams of sand running like water-courses down their centre. The camels followed each other, twisting in and out among the boulders, and scrambling with their adhesive, spongy feet over places which would have been impossible for horses. Among the broken rocks those behind could sometimes only see the long, undulating, darting necks of the creatures in front, as if it were some nightmare procession of serpents. Indeed, it had much the effect of a dream upon the prisoners, for there was no sound, save the soft, dull padding and shuffling of the feet. The strange, wild frieze moved slowly and silently onwards amid a setting of black stone and yellow sand, with the one arch of vivid blue spanning the rugged edges of the ravine.

Miss Adams, who had been frozen into silence during the long cold night, began to thaw now in the cheery warmth of the rising sun. She looked about her, and rubbed her thin hands together.

"Why, Sadie," she remarked, "I thought I heard you in the night, dear, and now I see that you have been crying."

"I've been thinking, auntie."

"Well, we must try and think of others, dearie, and not of ourselves."

"It's not of myself, auntie."

"Never fret about me, Sadie."

"No, auntie, I was not thinking of you."

"Was it of any one in particular?"

"Of Mr. Stephens, auntie. How gentle he was, and how brave! To think of him fixing up every little thing for us, and trying to pull his jacket over his poor roped-up hands, with those murderers waiting all round him. He's my saint and hero from now ever after."

"Well, he's out of his troubles anyhow," said Miss Adams, with that bluntness which the years bring with them.

"Then I wish I was also."

"I don't see how that would help him."

"Well, I think he might feel less lonesome," said Sadie, and drooped her saucy little chin upon her breast.

The four had been riding in silence for some little time, when the Colonel clapped his hand to his brow with a gesture of dismay.

"Good God!" he cried, "I am going off my head."

Again and again they had perceived it during the night, but he had seemed quite rational since daybreak. They were shocked therefore at this sudden outbreak, and tried to calm him with soothing words.

"Mad as a hatter," he shouted. "Whatever do you think I saw?"

"Don't trouble about it, whatever it was," said Mrs. Belmont, laying her hand soothingly upon his as the camels closed together. "It is no wonder that you are overdone. You have thought and worked for all of us so long. We shall halt presently, and a few hours' sleep will quite restore you."

But the Colonel looked up again, and again he cried out in his agitation and surprise.

"I never saw anything plainer in my life," he groaned. "It is on the point of rock on our right front—poor old Stuart with my red cummerbund round his head just the same as we left him."

The ladies had followed the direction of the Colonel's frightened gaze, and in an instant they were all as amazed as he.

There was a black, bulging ridge like a bastion upon the right side of the terrible khor up which the camels were winding. At one point it rose into a small pinnacle.

On this pinnacle stood a solitary, motionless figure, clad entirely in black, save for a brilliant dash of scarlet upon his head. There could not surely be two such short sturdy figures, or such large colourless faces, in the Libyan Desert. His shoulders were stooping forward, and he seemed to be staring intently down into the ravine. His pose and outline were like a caricature of the great Napoleon.

"Can it possibly be he?"

"It must be. It is!" cried the ladies. "You see he is looking towards us and waving his hand."

"Good Heavens! They'll shoot him! Get down, you fool, or you'll be shot!" roared the Colonel. But his dry throat would only emit a discordant croaking.

Several of the Dervishes had seen the singular apparition upon the hill, and had unslung their Remingtons, but a long arm suddenly shot up behind the figure of the Birmingham clergyman, a brown hand seized upon his skirts, and he disappeared with a snap. Higher up the pass, just below the spot where Mr. Stuart had been standing, appeared the tall figure of the Emir Abderrahman. He had sprung upon a boulder, and was shouting and waving his arms, but the shouts were drowned in a long, rippling roar of musketry from each side of the khor. The bastion-like cliff was fringed with gun-barrels, with red tarbooshes drooping over the triggers. From the other lip also came the long spurts of flame and the angry clatter of the rifles. The raiders were caught in an ambuscade. The Emir fell, but was up again and waving. There was a splotch of blood upon his long white beard. He kept pointing and gesticulating, but his scattered followers could not understand what he wanted. Some of them came tearing down the pass, and some from behind were pushing to the front. A few dismounted and tried to climb up sword in hand to that deadly line of muzzles, but one by one they were hit, and came rolling from rock to rock to the bottom of the ravine. The shooting was not very good. One negro made his way unharmed up the whole side, only to have his brains dashed out with the butt-end of a Martini at the top. The Emir had fallen off his rock and lay in a crumpled heap, like a brown and white patchwork quilt, at the bottom of it. And then when half of them were down it became evident, even to those exalted fanatical souls, that there was no chance for them, and that they must get out of these fatal rocks and into the desert again. They galloped down the pass, and it is a frightful thing to see a camel galloping over broken ground. The beast's own terror, his ungainly bounds, the sprawl of his four legs all in the air together, his hideous cries, and the yells of his rider who is bucked high from his saddle with every spring, make a picture which is not to be forgotten. The women screamed as this mad torrent of frenzied creatures came pouring past them, but the Colonel edged his camel and theirs farther and farther in among the rocks and away from the retreating Arabs. The air was full of whistling bullets, and they could hear them smacking loudly against the stones all round them.

"Keep quiet, and they'll pass us," whispered the Colonel, who was all himself again now that the hour for action had arrived. "I wish to Heaven I could see Tippy Tilly or any of his friends. Now is the time for them to help us." He watched the mad stream of fugitives as they flew past upon their shambling, squattering, loose-jointed beasts, but the black face of the Egyptian gunner was not among them.

And now it really did seem as if the whole body of them, in their haste to get clear of the ravine, had not a thought to spend upon the prisoners. The rush was past, and only stragglers were running the gauntlet of the fierce fire which poured upon them from above. The last of all, a young Baggara with a black moustache and pointed beard, looked up as he passed and shook his sword in impotent passion at the Egyptian riflemen. At the same instant a bullet struck his camel, and the creature collapsed, all neck and legs, upon the ground. The young Arab sprang off its back, and, seizing its nose-ring, he beat it savagely with the flat of his sword to make it stand up. But the dim, glazing eye told its own tale, and in desert warfare the death of the beast is the death of the rider. The Baggara glared round like a lion at bay, his dark eyes flashing murderously from under his red turban. A crimson spot, and then another, sprang out upon his dark skin, but he never winced at the bullet wounds. His fierce gaze had fallen upon the prisoners, and with an exultant shout he was dashing towards them, his broad-bladed sword gleaming above his head. Miss Adams was the nearest to him, but at the sight of the rushing figure and the maniac face she threw herself off the camel upon the far side. The Arab bounded on to a rock and aimed a thrust at Mrs. Belmont, but before the point could reach her the Colonel leaned forward with his pistol and blew the man's head in. Yet with a concentrated rage, which was superior even to the agony of death, the fellow lay kicking and striking, bounding about among the loose stones like a fish upon the shingle.

"Don't be frightened, ladies," cried the Colonel. "He is quite dead, I assure you. I am so sorry to have done this in your presence, but the fellow was dangerous. I had a little score of my own to settle with him, for he was the man who tried to break my ribs with his Remington. I hope you are not hurt, Miss Adams! One instant, and I will come down to you."

But the old Boston lady was by no means hurt, for the rocks had been so high that she had a very short distance to fall from her saddle. Sadie, Mrs. Belmont, and Colonel Cochrane had all descended by slipping on to the boulders and climbing down from them. But they found Miss Adams on her feet, and waving the remains of her green veil in triumph.

"Hurrah, Sadie! Hurrah, my own darling Sadie!" she was shrieking. "We are saved, my girl, we are saved after all."

"By George, so we are!" cried the Colonel, and they all shouted in an ecstasy together.

But Sadie had learned to think more about others during those terrible days of schooling. Her arms were round Mrs. Belmont, and her cheek against hers.

"You dear, sweet angel," she cried, "how can we have the heart to be glad when you—when you—"

"But I don't believe it is so," cried the brave Irishwoman. "No, I'll never believe it until I see John's body lying before me. And when I see that, I don't want to live to see anything more."

The last Dervish had clattered down the khor, and now above them on either cliff they could see the Egyptians—tall, thin, square shouldered figures, looking, when outlined against the blue sky, wonderfully like the warriors in the ancient bas-reliefs. Their camels were in the background, and they were hurrying to join them. At the same time others began to ride down from the farther end of the ravine, their dark faces flushed and their eyes shining with the excitement of victory and pursuit. A very small Englishman, with a straw-coloured moustache and a weary manner, was riding at the head of them. He halted his camel beside the fugitives and saluted the ladies. He wore brown boots and brown belts with steel buckles, which looked trim and workmanlike against his khaki uniform.

"Had 'em that time—had 'em proper!" said he. "Very glad to have been of any assistance, I'm sure. Hope you're none the worse for it all. What I mean, it's rather rough work for ladies."

"You're from Halfa, I suppose?" asked the Colonel.

"No, we're from the other show. We're the Sarras crowd, you know. We met in the desert, and we headed 'em off, and the other Johnnies herded 'em behind. We've got 'em on toast, I tell you. Get up on that rock and you'll see things happen. It's going to be a knockout in one round this time."

"We left some of our people at the Wells. We are very uneasy about them," said the Colonel. "I suppose you haven't heard anything of them?"

The young officer looked serious and shook his head. "Bad job that!" said he. "They're a poisonous crowd when you put 'em in a corner. What I mean, we never expected to see you alive, and we're very glad to pull any of you out of the fire. The most we hoped was that we might revenge you."

"Any other Englishman with you?"

"Archer is with the flanking party. He'll have to come past, for I don't think there is any other way down. We've got one of your chaps up there — a funny old bird with a red top-knot. See you later, I hope! Good day, ladies!" He touched his helmet, tapped his camel, and trotted on after his men.

"We can't do better than stay where we are until they are all past," said the Colonel, for it was evident now that the men from above would have to come round. In a broken single file they went past, black men and brown, Soudanese and fellaheen, but all of the best, for the Camel Corps is the corps d'elite of the Egyptian army. Each had a brown bandolier over his chest and his rifle held across his thigh. A large man with a drooping black moustache and a pair of binoculars in his hand was riding at the side of them. "Hulloa, Archer!" croaked the Colonel. The officer looked at him with the vacant, unresponsive eye of a complete stranger.

"I'm Cochrane, you know! We travelled up together."

"Excuse me, sir, but you have the advantage of me," said the officer. "I knew a Colonel Cochrane Cochrane, but you are not the man. He was three inches taller than you, with black hair and—"

"That's all right," cried the Colonel testily. "You try a few days with the Dervishes, and see if your friends will recognise you!"

"Good God, Cochrane, is it really you? I could not have believed it. Great Scott, what you must have been through! I've heard before of fellows going grey in a night, but, by Jove—"

"Quite so," said the Colonel, flushing.

"Allow me to hint to you, Archer, that if you could get some food and drink for these ladies, instead of discussing my personal appearance, it would be much more practical."

"That's all right," said Captain Archer. "Your friend Stuart knows that you are here, and he is bringing some stuff round for you. Poor fare, ladies, but the best we have! You're an old soldier, Cochrane. Get up on the rocks presently, and you'll see a lovely sight. No time to stop, for we shall be in action again in five minutes. Anything I can do before I go?"

"You haven't got such a thing as a cigar?" asked the Colonel wistfully.

Archer drew a thick satisfying partaga from his case, and handed it down, with half-a-dozen wax vestas. Then he cantered after his men, and the old soldier leaned back against the rock and drew in the fragrant smoke. It was then that his jangled nerves knew the full virtue of tobacco, the gentle anodyne which stays the failing strength and soothes the worrying brain. He watched the dim blue reek swirling up from him, and he felt the pleasant aromatic bite upon his palate, while a restful languor crept over his weary and harassed body. The three ladies sat together upon a flat rock.

"Good land, what a sight you are, Sadie!" cried Miss Adams suddenly, and it was the first reappearance of her old self. "What would your mother say if she saw you? Why, sakes alive, your hair is full of straw and your frock clean crazy!"

"I guess we all want some setting to rights," said Sadie, in a voice which was much more subdued than that of the Sadie of old. "Mrs. Belmont, you look just too perfectly sweet anyhow, but if you'll allow me I'll fix your dress for you."

But Mrs. Belmont's eyes were far away, and she shook her head sadly as she gently put the girl's hands aside.

"I do not care how I look. I cannot think of it," said she; "could you, if you had left the man you love behind you, as I have mine?"

"I'm begin—beginning to think I have," sobbed poor Sadie, and buried her hot face in Mrs. Belmont's motherly bosom.

X

The Camel Corps had all passed onwards down the khor in pursuit of the retreating Dervishes, and for a few minutes the escaped prisoners had been left alone. But now there came a cheery voice calling upon them, and a red turban bobbed about among the rocks, with the large white face of the Nonconformist minister smiling from beneath it. He had a thick lance with which to support his injured leg, and this murderous crutch combined with his peaceful appearance to give him a most incongruous aspect—as of a sheep which has suddenly developed claws. Behind him were two negroes with a basket and a water-skin.

"Not a word! Not a word!" he cried, as he stumped up to them. "I know exactly how you feel. I've been there myself. Bring the water, Ali! Only half a cup, Miss Adams;you shall have some more presently. Now your turn, Mrs. Belmont! Dear me, dear me, you poor souls, how my heart does bleed for you! There's bread and meat in the basket, but you must be very moderate at first." He chuckled with joy, and slapped his fat hands together as he watched them.

"But the others?" he asked, his face turning grave again.

The Colonel shook his head. "We left them behind at the wells. I fear that it is all over with them."

"Tut, tut!" cried the clergyman, in a boisterous voice, which could not cover the despondency of his expression; "you thought, no doubt, that it was all over with me, but here I am in spite of it. Never lose heart, Mrs. Belmont. Your husband's position could not possibly be as hopeless as mine was."

"When I saw you standing on that rock up yonder, I put it down to delirium," said the Colonel. "If the ladies had not seen you, I should never have ventured to believe it."

"I am afraid that I behaved very badly. Captain Archer says that I nearly spoiled all their plans, and that I deserved to be tried by a drumhead court-martial and shot. The fact is that, when I heard the Arabs beneath me, I forgot myself in my anxiety to know if any of you were left."

"I wonder that you were not shot without any drumhead court-martial," said the Colonel. "But how in the world did you get here?"

"The Halfa people were close upon our track at the time when I was abandoned, and they picked me up in the desert. I must have been delirious, I suppose, for they tell me that they heard my voice, singing hymns, a long way off, and it was that, under the providence of God, which brought them to me. They had a camel ambulance, and I was quite myself again by next day. I came with the Sarras people after we met them, because they have the doctor with them. My wound is nothing, and he says that a man of my habit will be the better for the loss of blood. And now, my friends"—his big, brown eyes lost their twinkle, and became very solemn and reverent—"we have all been upon the very confines of death, and our dear companions may be so at this instant. The same Power which saved us may save them, and let us pray together that it may be so, always remembering that if, in spite of our prayers, it should not be so, then that also must be accepted as the best and wisest thing."

So they knelt together among the black rocks, and prayed as some of them had never prayed before. It was very well to discuss prayer and treat it lightly and philosophically upon the deck of the Korosko. It was easy to feel strong and self-confident in the comfortable deck-chair, with the slippered Arab handing round the coffee and liqueurs. But they had been swept out of that placid stream of existence, and dashed against the horrible, jagged facts of life. Battered and shaken, they must have something to cling to. A blind, inexorable destiny was too horrible a belief. A chastening power, acting intelligently and for a purpose—a living, working power, tearing them out of their grooves, breaking down their small sectarian ways, forcing them into the better path—that was what they had learned to realise during these days of horror. Great hands had closed suddenly upon them, and had moulded them into new shapes, and fitted them for new uses. Could such a power be deflected by any human supplication? It was that or nothing—the last court of appeal, left open to injured humanity. And so they all prayed, as a lover loves, or a poet writes, from the very inside of their souls, and they rose with that singular, illogical feeling of inward peace and satisfaction which prayer only can give.

"Hush!" said Cochrane. "Listen!"

The sound of a volley came crackling up the narrow khor, and then another and another. The Colonel was fidgeting about like an old horse which hears the bugle of the hunt and the yapping of the pack.

"Where can we see what is going on?"

"Come this way! This way, if you please! There is a path up to the top. If the ladies will come after me, they will be spared the sight of anything painful."

The clergyman led them along the side to avoid the bodies which were littered thickly down the bottom of the khor. It was hard walking over the shingly, slaggy stones, but they made their way to the summit at last. Beneath them lay the vast expanse of the rolling desert, and in the foreground such a scene as none of them are ever likely to forget. In that perfectly dry and clear light, with the unvarying brown tint of the hard desert as a background, every detail stood out as clearly as if these were toy figures arranged upon a table within hand's-touch of them.

The Dervishes—or what was left of them—were riding slowly some little distance out in a confused crowd, their patchwork jibbehs and red turbans swaying with the motion of their camels. They did not present the appearance of men who were defeated, for their movements were very deliberate, but they looked about them and changed their formation as if they were uncertain what their tactics ought to be. It was no wonder that they were puzzled, for upon their spent camels their situation was as hopeless as could be conceived. The Sarras men had all emerged from the khor, and had dismounted, the beasts being held in groups of four, while the rifle-men knelt in a long line with a woolly, curling fringe of smoke, sending volley after volley at the Arabs, who shot back in a desultory fashion from the backs of their camels. But it was not upon the sullen group of Dervishes, nor yet upon the long line of kneeling rifle-men, that the eyes of the spectators were fixed. Far out upon the desert, three squadrons of the Halfa Camel Corps were coming up in a dense close column, which wheeled beautifully into a widespread semicircle as it approached. The Arabs were caught between two fires.

"By Jove!" cried the Colonel. "See that!"

The camels of the Dervishes had all knelt down simultaneously, and the men had sprung from their backs. In front of them was a tall, stately figure, who could only be the Emir Wad Ibrahim. They saw him kneel for an instant in prayer. Then he rose, and taking something from his saddle he placed it very deliberately upon the sand and stood upon it.

"Good man!" cried the Colonel. "He is standing upon his sheepskin."

"What do you mean by that?" asked Stuart.

"Every Arab has a sheepskin upon his saddle. When he recognises that his position is perfectly hopeless, and yet is determined to fight to the death, he takes his sheepskin off and stands upon it until he dies. See, they are all upon their sheepskins. They will neither give nor take quarter now."

The drama beneath them was rapidly approaching its climax. The Halfa Corps was well up, and a ring of smoke and flame surrounded the clump of kneeling Dervishes, who answered it as best they could. Many of them were already down, but the rest loaded and fired with the unflinching courage which has always made them worthy antagonists. A dozen khaki-dressed figures upon the sand showed that it was no bloodless victory for the Egyptians. But now there was a stirring bugle call from the Sarras men, and another answered it from the Halfa Corps. Their camels were down also, and the men had formed up into a single, long, curved line. One last volley, and they were charging inwards with the wild inspiriting yell which the blacks had brought with them from their central African wilds. For a minute there was a mad vortex of rushing figures, rifle butts rising and falling, spear-heads gleaming and darting among the rolling dust cloud. Then the bugle rang out once more, the Egyptians fell back and formed up with the quick precision of highly disciplined troops, and there in the centre, each upon his sheepskin, lay the gallant barbarian and his raiders. The nineteenth century had been revenged upon the seventh.

The three women had stared horror-stricken and yet fascinated at the stirring scene before them. Now Sadie and her aunt were sobbing together. The Colonel had turned to them with some cheering words when his eyes fell upon the face of Mrs. Belmont. It was as white and set as if it were carved from ivory, and her large grey eyes were fixed as if she were in a trance.

"Good Heavens, Mrs. Belmont, what is the matter?" he cried.

For answer she pointed out over the desert. Far away, miles on the other side of the scene of the fight, a small body of men were riding towards them.

"By Jove, yes; there's some one there. Who can it be?"

They were all straining their eyes, but the distance was so great that they could only be sure that they were camel-men and about a dozen in number.

"It's those devils who were left behind in the palm grove," said Cochrane. "There's no one else it can be. One consolation, they can't get away again. They've walked right into the lion's mouth."

But Mrs. Belmont was still gazing with the same fixed intensity, and the same ivory face. Now, with a wild shriek of joy, she threw her two hands into the air. "It's they!" she screamed. "They are saved! It's they, Colonel, it's they! Oh, Miss Adams, Miss Adams, it is they!" She capered about on the top of the hill with wild eyes like an excited child.

Her companions would not believe her, for they could see nothing, but there are moments when our mortal senses are more acute than those who have never put their whole heart and soul into them can ever realise. Mrs. Belmont had already run down the rocky path, on the way to her camel, before they could distinguish that which had long before carried its glad message to her. In the van of the approaching party, three white dots shimmered in the sun, and they could only come from the three European hats. The riders were travelling swiftly, and by the time their comrades had started to meet them they could plainly see that it was indeed Belmont, Fardet, and Stephens, with the dragoman Mansoor, and the wounded Soudanese rifleman. As they came together they saw that their escort consisted of Tippy Tilly and the other old Egyptian soldiers. Belmont rushed onwards to meet his wife, but Fardet stopped to grasp the Colonel's hand.

"Vive la France! Vivent les Anglais!" he was yelling. "Tout va bien, n'est ce pas, Colonel? Ah, canaille! Vivent la croix et les Chrétiens" He was incoherent in his delight.

The Colonel, too, was as enthusiastic as his Anglo-Saxon standard would permit. He could not gesticulate, but he laughed in the nervous crackling way which was his top-note of emotion.

"My dear boy, I am deuced glad to see you all again. I gave you up for lost. Never was as pleased at anything in my life! How did you get away?"

"It was all your doing."

"Mine?"

"Yes, my friend, and I have been quarrelling with you—ungrateful wretch that I am!"

"But how did I save you?"

"It was you who arranged with this excellent Tippy Tilly and the others that they should have so much if they brought us alive into Egypt again. They slipped away in the darkness and hid themselves in the grove. Then, when we were left, they crept up with their rifles and shot the men who were about to murder us. That cursed Moolah, I am sorry they shot him, for I believe that I could have persuaded him to be a Christian. And now, with your permission, I will hurry on and embrace Miss Adams, for Belmont has his wife, and Stephens has Miss Sadie, so I think it is very evident that the sympathy of Miss Adams is reserved for me."

A fortnight had passed away, and the special boat which had been placed at the disposal of the rescued tourists was already far north of Assiout. Next morning they would find themselves at Baliani, where one takes the express for Cairo. It was, therefore, their last evening together. Mrs. Shlesinger and her child, who had escaped unhurt, had already been sent down from the frontier. Miss Adams had been very ill after her privations, and this was the first time that she had been allowed to come upon deck after dinner. She sat now in a lounge chair, thinner, sterner, and kindlier than ever, while Sadie stood beside her and tucked the rugs around her shoulders. Mr. Stephens was carrying over the coffee and placing it on the wicker table beside them. On the other side of the deck Belmont and his wife were seated together in silent sympathy and contentment.

Monsieur Fardet was leaning against the rail, and arguing about the remissness of the British Government in not taking a more complete control of the Egyptian frontier, while the Colonel stood very erect in front of him, with the red end of a cigar-stump protruding from under his moustache.

But what was the matter with the Colonel? Who would have recognised him who had only seen the broken old man in the Libyan Desert? There might be some little grizzling about the moustache, but the hair was back once more at the fine glossy black which had been so much admired upon the voyage up. With a stony face and an unsympathetic manner he had received, upon his return to Halfa, all the commiserations about the dreadful way in which his privations had blanched him, and then diving into his cabin, he had reappeared within an hour exactly as he had been before that fatal moment when he had been cut off from the manifold resources of civilisation. And he looked in such a sternly questioning manner at every one who stared at him, that no one had the moral courage to make any remark about this modern miracle. It was observed from that time forward that, if the Colonel had only to ride a hundred yards into the desert, he always began his preparations by putting a small black bottle with a pink label into the side-pocket of his coat. But those who knew him best at times when a man may best be known, said that the old soldier had a young man's heart and a young man's spirit—so that if he wished to keep a young man's colour also it was not very unreasonable after all.

It was very soothing and restful up there on the saloon deck, with no sound but the gentle lipping of the water as it rippled against the sides of the steamer. The red after-glow was in the western sky, and it mottled the broad, smooth river with crimson. Dimly they could discern the tall figures of herons standing upon the sand-banks, and farther off the line of riverside date-palms glided past them in a majestic procession. Once more the silver stars were twinkling out, the same clear, placid, inexorable stars to which their weary eyes had been so often upturned during the long nights of their desert martyrdom.

"Where do you put up in Cairo, Miss Adams?" asked Mrs. Belmont at last.

"Shepheard's, I think."

"And you, Mr. Stephens?"

"Oh, Shepheard's, decidedly."

"We are staying at the Continental. I hope we shall not lose sight of you."

"I don't want ever to lose sight of you, Mrs. Belmont," cried Sadie. "Oh, you must come to the States, and we'll give you just a lovely time."

Mrs. Belmont laughed, in her pleasant, mellow fashion.

"We have our duty to do in Ireland, and we have been too long away from it already. My husband has his business, and I have my home, and they are both going to rack and ruin. Besides," she added slyly, "it is just possible that if we did come to the States we might not find you there."

"We must all meet again," said Belmont, "if only to talk our adventures over once more. It will be easier in a year or two. We are still too near them. "

"And yet how far away and dream-like it all seems!" remarked his wife. "Providence is very good in softening disagreeable remembrances in our minds. All this feels to me as if it had happened in some previous existence."

Fardet held up his wrist with a cotton bandage still round it.

"The body does not forget as quickly as the mind. This does not look very dream-like or far away, Mrs. Belmont."

"How hard it is that some should be spared, and some not! If only Mr. Brown and Mr. Headingly were with us, then I should not have one care in the world," cried Sadie. "Why should they have been taken, and we left?"

Mr. Stuart had limped on to the deck withan open book in his hand, a thick stick supporting his injured leg.

"Why is the ripe fruit picked, and the unripe left?" said he in answer to the young girl's exclamation. "We know nothing of the spiritual state of these poor dear young fellows, but the great Master Gardener plucks His fruit according to His own knowledge. I brought you up a passage to read to you."

There was a lantern upon the table, and he sat down beside it. The yellow light shone upon his heavy cheek and the red edges of his book. The strong, steady voice rose above the wash of the water.

"'Let them give thanks whom the Lord hath redeemed and delivered from the hand of the enemy, and gathered them out of the lands, from the east, and from the west, from the north, and from the south. They went astray in the wilderness out of the way, and found no city to dwell in. Hungry and thirsty, their soul fainted in them. So they cried unto the Lord in their trouble, and He delivered them from their distress. He led them forth by the right way, that they might go to the city where they dwelt. Oh that men would therefore praise the Lord for His goodness, and declare the wonders that He doeth for the children of men.'

"It sounds as if it were composed for us, and yet it was written two thousand years ago," said the clergyman, as he closed the book. "In every age man has been forced to acknowledge the guiding hand which leads him. For my part I don't believe that inspiration stopped two thousand years ago. When Tennyson wrote with such fervour and conviction":—

'Oh, yet we trust that somehow good Will be the final goal of ill,'

"He was repeating the message which had been given to him, just as Micah or Ezekiel, when the world was younger, repeated some cruder and more elementary message."

"That is all very well, Mr. Stuart," said the Frenchman; "you ask me to praise God for taking me out of danger and pain, but what I want to know is why, since He has arranged all things, He ever put me into that pain and danger. I have, in my opinion, more occasion to blame than to praise. You would not thank me for pulling you out of that river if it was also I who pushed you in. The most which you can claim for your Providence is that it has healed the wound which its own hand inflicted."

"I don't deny the difficulty," said the clergyman slowly; "no one who is not self-deceived can deny the difficulty. Look how boldly Tennyson faced it in that same poem, the grandest and deepest and most obviously inspired in our language. Remember the effect which it had upon him."

'I falter where I firmly trod, And falling with my weight of cares Upon the great world's altar stairs Which slope through darkness up to God;

I stretch lame hands of faith and grope And gather dust and chaff, and call To what I feel is Lord of all, And faintly trust the larger hope.'

"It is the central mystery of mysteries—the problem of sin and suffering, the one huge difficulty which the reasoner has to solve in order to vindicate the dealings of God with man. But take our own case as an example. I, for one, am very clear what I have got out of our experience. I say it with all humility, but I have a clearer view of my duties than ever I had before. It has taught me to be less remiss in saying what I think to be true, less indolent in doing what I feel to be right."

"And I," cried Sadie. "It has taught me more than all my life put together. I have learned so much and unlearned so much. I am a different girl. "

"I never understood my own nature before," said Stephens. "I can hardly say that I had a nature to understand. I lived for what was unimportant, and I neglected what was vital."

"Oh, a good shake-up does nobody any harm," the Colonel remarked. "Too much of the feather-bed-and-four-meals-a-day life is not good for man or woman. "

"It is my firm belief," said Mrs. Belmont gravely, "that there was not one of us who did not rise to a greater height during those days in the desert than ever before or since. When our sins come to be weighed, much may be forgiven us for the sake of those unselfish days."

They all sat in thoughtful silence for a little, while the scarlet streaks turned to carmine, and the grey shadows deepened, and the wild-fowl flew past in dark straggling V's over the dull metallic surface of the great smooth-flowing Nile. A cold wind had sprung up from the eastward, and some of the party rose to leave the deck. Stephens leaned forward to Sadie.

"Do you remember what you promised when you were in the desert?" he whispered.

"What was that?"

"You said that if you escaped you would try in future to make some one else happy."

"Then I must do so."

"You have," said he, and their hands met under the shadow of the table.

18858282R00070

Printed in Great Britain
by Amazon